*Surely she*

Unable to help herself, Molly relived each stroke, each caress, each heated kiss until she missed Chase so badly she wanted to tell him she'd been wrong.

But she knew better than that.

With each second that silently tick-tocked through the room, time stretched and strained like a frayed rubber band, tighter and tighter until it was ready to snap.

Finally, a little pink dot formed, mocking every attempt Molly had made to convince herself she hadn't conceived. She blinked her eyes a couple of times, hoping to clear her vision, hoping to see that the result screen had remained blank.

But that bright pink spot wasn't going anywhere.

Molly sat on the commode for the longest time, peering at the testing apparatus and hoping for a different outcome until she was forced to accept the truth.

She was pregnant—with Chase Mayfield's baby.

Dear Reader,

Summer is a perfect time to read. With all the books available to you, I'm glad you chose *Race to the Altar,* the first story in my BRIGHTON VALLEY MEDICAL CENTER series.

Those who enjoyed reading THE TEXAS HOMECOMING books will get a chance to return to Brighton Valley and experience a medical setting this time around. But don't worry. You'll meet a few cowboys and ranchers, too!

I love a good western—whether it's a book, a movie or a song—and that's why many of my romances have a Texas setting. So grab a glass of sweet tea—or maybe a sarsaparilla—and escape to Brighton Valley for a guaranteed happy ending.

When you finish *Race to the Altar,* be sure to visit my Web site, www.JudyDuarte.com, and let me know what you thought of the story and the setting. I'd love to hear from you.

Wishing you romance,

*Judy Duarte*

# RACE TO
# THE ALTAR

## *JUDY DUARTE*

Published by Silhouette Books

**America's Publisher of Contemporary Romance**

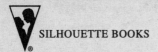

SILHOUETTE BOOKS

ISBN-13: 978-0-373-65471-0

RACE TO THE ALTAR

Recycling programs
for this product may
not exist in your area.

Visit Silhouette Books at www.eHarlequin.com

**Printed in U.S.A.**

**Books by Judy Duarte**

Silhouette Special Edition

*Cowboy Courage* #1458
*Family Practice* #1511
*Almost Perfect* #1540
*Big Sky Baby* #1563
*The Virgin's Makeover* #1593
*Bluegrass Baby* #1598
*The Rich Man's Son* #1634
\*Hailey's Hero #1659
\*Their Secret Son #1667
*Their Unexpected Family* #1676
\*Worth Fighting For #1684
\*The Matchmakers' Daddy #1689

*His Mother's Wedding* #1731
*Call Me Cowboy* #1743
\*\*The Perfect Wife #1773
*Rock-a-Bye Rancher* #1784
*Daddy on Call* #1822
*The Cowboy's Lullaby* #1834
††*Romancing the Cowboy* #1888
§*Once Upon a Pregnancy* #1891
††*In Love with the Bronc Rider* #1907
††*Her Best Christmas Ever* #1943
§§*A Real Live Cowboy* #1964
‡*Race to the Altar* #1989

Silhouette Books

‡*Double Destiny*
"Second Chance"

\*Bayside Bachelors
\*\*Talk of the Neighborhood
††The Texas Homecoming
§The Wilder Family
§§Fortunes of Texas:
     Return to Red Rock
‡Brighton Valley Medical Center

## *JUDY DUARTE*

always knew there was a book inside her, but since English was her least favorite subject in school, she never considered herself a writer. An avid reader who enjoyed a happy ending, Judy couldn't shake the dream of creating a book of her own.

Her dream became a reality in March of 2002, when Silhouette Special Edition released her first book, *Cowboy Courage.* Since then, her stories have touched the hearts of readers around the world. In July of 2005, Judy won the prestigious Readers' Choice Award for *The Rich Man's Son.*

You can write to Judy c/o Silhouette Books, 233 Broadway, Suite 1001, New York, NY 10237. You can also contact her at JudyDuarte@sbcglobal.net, or through her Web site, www.judyduarte.com.

To the members
of the San Diego chapter of Romance Writers of America
for your friendship and support over the years,
as well as the wealth of knowledge I've gleaned
from your awesome workshops. You rock.

# *Chapter One*

Chase Mayfield left his sponsors in the den of the sprawling ranch house and headed for the front door, his temper just barely under control.

What the hell had that been? Some sort of intervention?

When he'd been summoned to the gentleman's ranch owned by Texas oilman Gerald Barden, he hadn't given it a second thought. He'd figured the men wanted to discuss the racing schedule, the competition and what they expected from their driver in the upcoming season, so he'd been surprised when they'd laid down the law about how he would conduct himself off the track from now on.

But Chase didn't like ultimatums—never had, never would.

Outside, the stars flickered overhead, and like the

restless spirit that often swept through him, a warm summer breeze stirred up the leaves on the ground.

He wished he could kick that edgy spirit that had been a part of him since he'd been in diapers and had toddled after his older brothers, but he'd never been able to.

After climbing into the classic '63 Corvette he'd recently restored, Chase turned the ignition and pumped the gas pedal. When the engine responded with a well-tuned roar, he put the transmission into gear and started the long drive back to Houston, hoping to put some distance between him and his sponsors.

Chase had always lived life in the fast lane, both on and off the track. Hell, he didn't know how to live any other way; he didn't even want to.

Besides, he'd had his fill of people bossing him around while he was growing up. By the time he hit his teen years, he'd decided not to put up with it anymore.

For that reason alone, he was tempted to flip open his cell phone, call Gerald Barden back at the ranch and tell him and his cronies what they could do with their money. But he figured it was best to let things ride for a while. After all, Chase didn't have any other burning interests that left him many options.

Of course, settling down wasn't much of an option, either. Marriage certainly hadn't tamed the restlessness that plagued him, and neither had racing. Divorce might have ended his marriage, but racing and competition were in his blood.

Once on the open highway, Chase again pondered the ultimatum he'd been given.

"You're going to have to stay out of trouble and bars,"

Gerald had said. "We don't like the press you've been getting, son. If you don't fly under the media radar, you can kiss our money goodbye."

He'd wanted to remind Gerald and the others that he'd been racking up points and bringing them the kind of success they'd been hoping for. But over the years he'd gotten to know Gerald better than the man might even know himself—and he'd learned when to push his point and when to keep his mouth shut.

And this had clearly been a keep-your-mouth-shut night.

"Family's important to us," Gerald had tossed in for good measure.

It was important to Chase, too, but he doubted if anyone believed him. He hadn't been back home in ages. But he hadn't been up for an argument with the men who signed the checks. Not tonight.

About thirty-five minutes into his drive, he noticed a sign that said Now Entering Brighton Valley.

That wasn't right. Had he made a wrong turn? Where the hell was the county road?

A block ahead, a nearly burned-out neon bulb in a streetlight flickered, limiting his vision. He caught sight of several trash cans sitting curbside.

Chase glanced farther up the road, noting a big rig coming down the opposite side of the street.

Just as he realized he would need to make a U-turn so he could get back on the route to Houston, a small animal—a cat or a dog maybe?—darted out in the street, followed by a larger blur of pink. A child?

Chase had always been ready for the unexpected,

especially on the road, but at this time of night he hadn't expected to see a kid playing outside. He hit the brakes, all the while watching the blonde pixie caught in the high beam of his headlights freeze, her eyes wide, her mouth gaped, her pink nightgown billowing and revealing bare feet.

His first reaction had been to pull to the right, but when another child on a bicycle whizzed into his path, the only choice he had was to turn sharply to the left, hoping to broadside the semi rather than hit it head-on.

He gripped the steering wheel as adrenaline pumped through him and threw his mind into slow-motion mode.

With no air bags, no roll bar and only a fiberglass car body, this crash wasn't going to be as easy to walk away from as the others had been.

Upon impact, pain exploded in his head, and then everything went black.


Molly Edwards sat at the nurses' desk in the emergency room at Brighton Valley Medical Center, hoping Karen Wylie would arrive and relieve her soon. Normally, Molly didn't work in the E.R.—or work the night shift, for that matter—but Karen had called in with some kind of family emergency, saying she'd be a couple of hours late.

Since the new hospital was struggling to stay afloat financially, there'd been a hiring freeze and the staff was stretched to the limit. So here Molly was, covering for Karen and holding down the E.R. fort.

There was one good thing about working in emergency, though. It was usually busy, and time flew by. But so far this evening had been fairly quiet.

Earlier, a couple of cowboys had come in after a friendly card game devolved into a brawl. None of the men had been injured seriously in the fight, but one had suffered chest pains and was now on the second floor, where he was being treated by the resident cardiologist.

A toddler who'd had a febrile seizure was in one of the pediatric beds, but he would be going home soon. Dr. Betsy Bramblett—or rather, *Nielson*—had tried to assure the worried parents that a sudden spike in temperature could cause convulsions in a small child, and that this particular type of seizure wasn't as dangerous as it might seem.

Dawn McGregor, the nurse who'd answered the phone moments ago, was sitting to the right of Molly, jotting down notes. When she ended her communication with paramedics en route to the hospital, she got to her feet. "Get ready for another accident victim. A guy driving a sports car collided with a semi truck. The trucker's fine, just a little shook up. He declined treatment, but the sports car driver has a head injury, lacerations and possible fractures."

Molly couldn't help but wince. She hated dealing with the aftermath of a car accident, especially in a triage setting. Twelve years ago, when she was seventeen, she'd lost her parents and her brother in a head-on collision.

After a high school football game, they'd left San Antonio and were headed to Brighton Valley to visit her grandparents. Along the way, a reckless driver had run a red light and careened into the family minivan. Her father had died upon impact, and her mother had been DOA. Jimmy, her younger brother, had clung to life for nearly two days before he died from his injuries, leaving Molly as the only survivor.

She'd been injured, of course, but not seriously. For some inexplicable reason the corner of the backseat where she'd been dozing with her favorite pillow had been spared the brunt of the impact. Most people had called it a miracle, but she tended to see it as a weird twist of fate that had spared her rather than the others.

For the longest time she'd felt guilty—for insisting they leave when they did, for sleeping through it, for practically walking away from it. She'd also been devastated by the loss, but she'd eventually worked through the grief, thanks to the love and support of her grandparents.

Two years later, when Gramps suffered a heart attack, which—thank God—hadn't been fatal, the hospital experience had had a positive effect on Molly. She'd gained a real appreciation for healthcare professionals during her visits to him, and soon after he was discharged she'd decided to pursue a nursing degree, hoping to be able to help people in pain and to comfort families who were suffering. It gave her a purpose, a reason to be alive.

While she no longer let her own personal tragedy drag her down, she had to admit it was the main reason she didn't work in the E.R. on a regular basis—too many feelings of déjà vu.

Molly closed the chart she'd been working on and scanned the room to see if Karen had clocked in yet. She hoped so, because she was eager to go home and get some sleep before returning to the hospital to start her shift at 6:00 a.m. But Karen was nowhere in sight, which meant Molly would be called upon to help with the incoming accident victim.

Oh, well. It was all in a day's work.

"What's the victim's ETA?" Molly asked Dawn.

"Three minutes, maybe less."

"Thanks. I'll give Dr. Nielson a heads-up."

Dawn handed Molly the slip of paper on which she'd written the patient's vitals, including blood pressure, respiration, pulse rate and other pertinent details.

Molly took note of it all as she headed toward the toddler's bed. She glanced up in time to see Betsy Nielson draw aside the blue privacy curtain and leave the child's bedside.

"Doctor," Molly said, "we have a car accident victim coming in—a male, twenty-nine years old and unconscious. He has lacerations, possible fractures and a head injury. The ETA is approximately two minutes."

"All right. Only one victim?"

"Yes, the driver of a Corvette. The trucker wasn't hurt."

The doctor and nurse made their way to the triage area, and moments later the automatic door swung open. Two EMTs rushed in with the patient on a gurney, and the E.R. staff kicked into high gear.

Molly had been expecting the worst, and she'd been right. The driver of the sports car was still unconscious. His eyes were bruised and swollen, and blood from a laceration over his left brow covered most of his face.

Since Karen would be relieving her soon, she stepped back to allow Dawn to join the doctor, then worked with the paramedics as they recited their findings and their treatment en route.

Dr. Nielson, whom Molly referred to as Betsy when they weren't working, listened intently while she made a methodical assessment of the man's injuries.

"Cut off his clothes," Betsy told Dawn, as the two continued to examine the patient.

When the transfer of information was complete, Molly turned to the E.R. drama unfolding and watched Dr. Nielson work. Even with the blood cleaned from his battered face, it was difficult to imagine what he'd looked like before the collision. Handsome, she suspected. And she couldn't quell her curiosity about him.

Joe Villa, the ambulance driver, handed Molly a plastic bag holding the man's wallet. "His ID says his name is Chase Mayfield. I wonder if he's the race car driver."

Molly wouldn't know. She didn't follow sports and wasn't into cars. In fact, ever since the accident, she'd been uneasy whenever she got behind the wheel.

She did, of course, own a car, but she preferred to ride her bike around town, saving the vehicle to use on rainy days.

"It's hard to imagine a celebrity like that being in Brighton Valley," Sheila Conway, the senior EMT, said.

"Yes, but he was driving a classic old Corvette," Joe reminded her. "That tells me he appreciates speed and a fast car."

"Maybe so." Sheila crossed her arms. "But he won't be zipping around town in that Corvette anymore. It's little more than a mangled mess now."

Molly hadn't recognized the name at all, so it was anyone's guess if he was the same guy.

If he really was a race car driver, one thing that she did know was that he was a man who normally cheated death on the track. A man who had no fear. Or, if he did, he'd learned to control it.

Unable to help herself, she opened the plastic bag and pulled out Chase's ID. His driver's license photo wasn't all that remarkable, but then most of them weren't.

His black, unruly curls were matted with blood now. And his eyes, which his ID said were blue, were swollen shut.

What had they looked like before?

According to his ID, he was six feet tall, a hundred and ninety pounds. He had a birthday coming on October seventeenth.

He'd be thirty. But that's about all she could assess, other than he'd probably been an attractive man when he'd started out today.

Her curiosity continued to build, which was strange. Normally she kept a professional distance from her patients, yet for some reason she was drawn to this one. And that was crazy, since there were several good reasons to excuse herself now that the paramedics were packing up and preparing to leave.

"By the way," Sheila added, "there's a kid coming in, too. He has a laceration on his left leg which may need stitches, as well as a possible fracture of the wrist. His guardian is driving him in."

"Was he involved in the accident?" Molly asked.

"He was looking for his little sister, who'd chased

after a runaway cat. When he saw the collision, he lost his balance and fell off his bike."

Molly nodded, then returned her attention to the man on the gurney—Chase Mayfield.

"He's coming to," Betsy said. "Hi, Chase. You're in a hospital. You've been in an accident. I'm Dr. Nielson. How are you feeling?"

He grimaced.

"Your injuries aren't life threatening," Betsy told him, "but we're going to run a few tests. We also want to keep you in the ICU tonight for observation."

His only response was a moan.

Betsy went on to probe and clean his head wound. After telling him what she was about to do, she began stitching it shut.

Dawn, who'd ordered an MRI, reentered the room just as Betsy finished the last of ten or twelve sutures over Chase's left eye. "Doctor, the boy arrived and is waiting with his guardian."

Betsy nodded. "I'll be finished here in a few minutes."

The man moaned again.

"Chase?" Betsy asked.

No response.

"Wake up, Mr. Mayfield."

Chase cracked open his good eye. "Where… what…?"

"You're in the hospital," Betsy told him again. "You were involved in an accident. Do you remember?"

He seemed to be trying to process the information. "Oh…yeah."

"Can you tell me what happened?" the doctor asked.

Molly knew Betsy wasn't interested in details of the accident. She was actually trying to assess the extent of his head injury and his cognitive function.

"A dog…a kid…a truck…" His eyes opened momentarily, then closed again. "I had to pick one…"

He'd opted for the truck, Molly concluded.

"Good choice," Betsy said. "At least, for the sake of the kid and the dog."

Chase grumbled. Or perhaps it was a groan.

"Rumor has it you might be *the* Chase Mayfield," Betsy said. "The race car driver."

"Rumor has a big mouth."

So, Molly thought, he had a sense of humor. And apparently, he *was* the man in question. She drew closer to the bed. "Karen still hasn't arrived, Doctor. So I can finish cleaning him up and put on his gown."

"Thanks, Molly. I really appreciate you coming in to pinch hit like this."

"No problem." She glanced at the patient.

He opened his eyes. Well, actually, he opened the one that wasn't completely swelled shut, and it was the prettiest shade of blue Molly had ever seen. Like the color of the stone in her mother's sapphire ring.

"We can transport you to Houston," Betsy told him, "if you'd rather be in a larger hospital."

"No." Chase turned to the doctor and reached out, grabbing Molly's arm by mistake, gripping her with an intensity that shot her adrenaline through the roof. "I don't want to go to the city."

"No problem," the doctor said. "You can stay here, if you'd rather."

"I don't—" he winced "—want word to get out… about this…if it can be helped."

"We'll do what we can to ensure your privacy," Betsy assured him. "But there were witnesses to the accident. The media could find out, although we certainly won't make any statements, if that's what you're concerned about."

"I want to…fly under the radar." He opened his eye a crack. "Use my middle name, Raymond, instead of Chase. Maybe that'll throw people off."

"We'll issue a request for discretion." Betsy turned to Molly. "I'll let you take it from here. I'll order some Demerol and let ICU know he's on his way up."

"All right."

Chase closed his eyes and blew out a sigh.

"Is there someone I can call for you?" Molly asked. "Someone who's expecting you at home?"

"No." He blew out another ragged breath. "Damn, my head…hurts."

"Dr. Nielson is ordering pain meds. I'll go and get it for you."

Ten minutes later, after giving Chase an injection, Molly had managed to fill out the forms and have Mr. Mayfield formally admitted to the hospital—under his middle name, Raymond.

She'd returned to his bedside to tell him, but he'd fallen asleep—his eyes were shut, his breathing even.

Good, she thought. He'd feel better in dreamland.

She reached into the cupboard and took out one of the hospital gowns. Then she proceeded to pull down the sheet to Chase's waist, noting the broad shoulders, the sprinkle of dark hair across his chest, the well-defined abs, the…

Oh, wow. The whisper of a sexual rush buzzed through her veins, and she did her best to shake it off.

She'd seen countless naked men in her life—professionally speaking, of course—but she'd never had a purely feminine response to a patient.

Until this moment.

Doing her best to ignore the unwelcome physical reaction, she slipped his arms through the gown, then proceeded to lift his shoulder just enough to tie at least one of the strings.

"Ow. What're you doing?"

Startled, she gently rolled him back on the mattress. "Getting you dressed."

Did he realize his nakedness had unbalanced her?

Surely not.

"You dozed for a few minutes," she said, trying to get her mind back on track. "How are you feeling now?"

"Like I…got hit by a…Mack truck."

"I think you did." She smiled at his joke, letting down her guard just a little. "A sense of humor should help you recover quickly, so I'm glad your funny bone wasn't fractured."

"What do you know? A pretty nurse…and witty, too. I…like that…in a woman." He managed a faint smile.

She couldn't help but wonder what one of his smiles would have looked like before his face had been swollen and bruised.

His eyes—well, the one that had actually opened—

closed again. She hoped that meant he was really drifting off to la-la land.

She sure hoped so. She really needed to be done with this shift, done with him. She didn't like the unprofessional turn her thoughts had taken. So she straightened, eager to pass him on to another nurse. One who knew how to keep her feminine side in check.

Before she could pull the curtain aside, Betsy peeked in on them. "How's he doing?"

"I'd say he's on the road to mend."

"Good. If all goes well in ICU tonight, we'll be sending him to the third floor in the morning."

So much for being able to pass him off to someone else. That's where Molly would be tomorrow, and with her luck, she'd probably be assigned to his room for at least part of the time he was in the hospital. Unless, of course, she could figure out a way to talk her way out of it.

"I promised to do what I could to protect his identity from the media," Betsy said. "So I'm reluctant to let anyone else come in close contact with him."

"How are you going to do that?"

"I'm going to suggest that he be assigned to you for the entire time he's here. That should be the easiest way to maintain confidentiality."

Molly tried not to roll her eyes or object. "How long do you expect that to be?"

"A week maybe, unless there are complications." Betsy's gaze intensified. "Do you have a problem with this, Molly?"

"No, not at all." She was a professional. She did her job and took care of whatever patient had been assigned to her.

It's just that this patient was different. According to the paramedics who'd brought him in, he'd been speeding and had, at least indirectly, caused a young boy to be injured. So Chase and his accident brought back a painful sense of déjà vu.

She could deal with that, she supposed.

As she walked around to the side of the gurney, kicking off the brake, he reached out and clamped a hand on her wrist. The hint of a smile crossed his battered face. "No speeding, okay?"

"I'll keep it under a hundred," she said as she maneuvered the gurney out the door and into the hall.

"Be careful," he said. "I don't like to ride in the passenger seat."

Interestingly enough, neither did Molly. She'd been asleep when her family's minivan had spun out of control and ran off the road, unable to shout out a warning or grab the wheel.

Not a day went by that she didn't ask herself what would have happened if she'd been the one driving, if she'd been alert instead of asleep. Would she have been able to steer clear of an accident?

Would her family be alive today?

She guessed she would never know for sure, but either way, she didn't trust anyone behind the wheel except herself.

"Are you married?" he asked.

"No."

"Got a boyfriend?"

"Not at the moment." She glanced down at the battered face of her victim, wondering if he was flirting with her or if the concussion and the Demerol were making him chatty.

"Guess that makes it my lucky day," he said.

"It wasn't lucky earlier." She couldn't help chuckling as she pushed the gurney down the hall.

"How's the kid?" he asked.

"Which one?"

"Both, I guess."

From what she understood, a little girl had dashed outside and into the street, chasing after a cat that ran away. And her brother went after her on his bicycle. "You didn't hit either of them. The girl is fine, and her brother fell off his bike. He may have broken his wrist, but nothing serious."

As Molly continued pushing the gurney toward the elevator that would take them to ICU, one of the wheels froze then wobbled.

"Watch it," he said. "One accident tonight is all I can handle."

"Don't worry. I'll be very careful." And she wasn't just talking about transporting him through the hospital corridors. Whether she was willing to admit it or not, she found herself drawn to the race car driver whose lifestyle should be a great big turn-off to a woman who didn't like to take any unnecessary risks. A patient who'd been battered in an automobile wreck and whose cuts and bruises ought to make him completely unattractive.

So what was with the unexpected feminine interest in Chase Mayfield, a man sure to make her life miserable?

## Chapter Two

Chase had no idea what time he'd been transported from the ICU to a room on the third floor, but since the sun was pouring through his window, damn near blinding him, he knew it was well after dawn.

He'd had to ask the tall, spindly orderly who'd brought him here to pull the blinds so his head wouldn't explode.

As soon as the room had been darkened and Chase could see out of his good eye, he searched for the blonde nurse who'd undressed him last night. If she'd worn a name tag, he hadn't noticed, but he suspected he would recognize her if he saw her again—no matter how lousy his vision was.

As he looked around, he spotted a TV, a tray table and a monitor of some kind, but Blondie was nowhere in sight. Instead, another, rather nondescript nurse came to check on him, pour him water and point out the TV remote and the call button, as if he gave a squat about all that now.

"Can I get you anything else?" she asked.

He didn't suspect a new head was possible. "No, I'm okay."

Moments later he dozed off again, only to be awakened by a male nurse who was the size of a Dallas Cowboys linebacker.

Or had there been two of them merging into one?

"Raymond?" one or both of them asked.

"Yeah, that's me." Chase blinked and looked again. Okay, it was just one guy, and maybe he wasn't all that big after all.

"I've come to get some blood, Raymond."

Maybe it was the man's quest for blood, but Chase could have sworn he'd detected a Bela Lugosi accent and wondered if he ought to have someone bring him some garlic.

No, it had to be the Demerol they'd given him. If Bela started flying through his room or hanging upside down from the ceiling, he'd have to refuse any more shots.

Chase lifted his arm about an inch off the bed, then let it drop to the mattress. "I'd help, but my body isn't at a hundred percent."

"No problem." Bela placed a blue plastic tote box full of lab paraphernalia on the tray table. Next he took a green band of rubber, wrapped it around the top of Chase's arm and twisted until it pinched. Then he jabbed and poked at a vein a couple of times until he finally struck blood. "There. That wasn't too bad, was it?"

"Bad enough." Chase's head hurt like hell, and every bone in his body felt as though it had been run over by a steamroller. A needle stabbing into his arm just added insult to injury.

If he'd been at all able, he would have busted out of here and gone home to Houston, but as it was he had about as much fight left in him as a baby bunny.

After Bela left, a wave of nausea swept through him, turning his stomach inside out. He wondered if he ought to ring for the nurse. Instead, he decided to wait it out, knowing that he was having a hard time staying awake anyway.

He'd no more than faded off again when someone came in with a tray of food and announced it was lunchtime. It was a teenage girl with her brown hair in a ponytail and wearing a pink-and-white-striped dress. She took the plastic domed lid off a plate, sending a smorgasbord of fumes straight to his nostrils.

"Oh, God," he said.

"Do you need some help?"

"Yeah. Take it away. Just looking at it makes me feel like I'm going to puke."

"I'll tell your nurse. Maybe they can give you something for that."

Whatever.

The next time Chase heard footsteps he cracked open an eye, the one that actually worked, and caught sight of the pretty blonde nurse who'd worked on him last night.

"Chase?" she asked.

"Call me Raymond. And if you told me your name, I've forgotten."

"I'm Molly, and I'll be your nurse today. How are you feeling?"

He turned his head toward the lull of her voice, only to feel a sharp pull in his neck. "Like hell. But maybe I'll recover now that you're back. That other nurse—Bela or whatever his name is—has it in for me."

"His name is Eric, and he's a lab tech." She neared his bed, took his wrist in her fingers and felt for a pulse. "What makes you think he doesn't like you?"

"He kept stabbing me with a dull needle."

"Sometimes the veins are hard to find."

Chase grimaced, then tried to roll to his side and reach for the bed rail. "Ow. Damn, that hurts."

"What's the matter?"

"I'm going to need help getting to the bathroom."

"I don't think Dr. Nielson wants you up yet. I'll get you a bedpan."

"Don't bother. I'd rather hold it until my eyes turn yellow than use one of those again." Especially with Nurse Molly holding it.

She smiled, and her eyes—green or blue? It was hard to tell with impaired vision—glimmered. "We can try a catheter."

"Not if you want to live to tell about it."

She laughed, a melodious lilt that at any other time might have charmed his socks off. But now? Well, the pain and the whole damn situation had done a number on his sense of humor. But he had to admit that the blonde Florence Nightingale beat the heck out of Bela or the candy striper.

"I'll call one of the male nurses or an orderly to come and help," she said.

He'd never had what they call a shy bladder, but something told him that might even be worse.

"How long have I been in this room?" he asked. "It feels like a week."

Molly looked at her wristwatch, a no-nonsense type with a leather band. "About forty-five minutes."

She walked to a whiteboard on the wall, pulled out a black marker and wrote her first name, followed by a phone number. "This is my pager number. The call button will bring anyone at the nurses' desk. But if you need me, give me a call, and I'll come as soon as I can."

That seemed easy enough.

"I know that you wanted to 'fly under the radar,'" she said, "but are you sure there isn't someone we should tell that you're here? Parents, sister, girlfriend, neighbor?"

"Not unless I'm dying."

"No pets at the house that need to be fed?" she asked.

"Nope." He turned his head toward her, even though it hurt his neck to do so. "Are you just a soft-hearted nurse? Or are you trying to ask in a subtle way if I'm attached?"

"Actually, you're not all that attractive right now. And any sign of personality or charm is nonexistent. So, no, I wasn't quizzing you for personal reasons."

"Too bad." He tossed her a painfully crooked grin, sorry that he wasn't at his best and wondering what she saw when she looked at him.

* * *

Molly studied her battered patient, trying to imagine the photo on the ID she'd seen last night—dark, curly hair that hadn't been matted from bed rest, expressive blue eyes that actually opened and blinked.

If she knew what was good for her, she'd be a lot more focused on what he looked like now. A nurse had no business being attracted to her patient. And Molly, especially, didn't need to be intrigued by a race car driver who'd probably had more than his share of women.

Yet she couldn't help getting involved in a little flirtatious banter. "So what's a nice guy like you doing in a place like this?"

"Are you trying to hit on me?" There was the hint of a grin on his face.

Molly laughed. "Sorry. I'm not into the footloose, reckless type. I was just trying to make conversation."

"Too bad," he said. "It would be nice to have my own private duty nurse, especially a pretty blonde."

"Something tells me, with your occupation, you probably ought to have your own mobile medical unit."

"Actually, I'm a very good driver."

She crossed her arms, a smile stealing across her face. "Those lumps and cuts and bruises suggest otherwise."

"It could have been worse."

A lot worse. He could have died—or one of the children could have.

As though reading her thoughts, he asked, "So how's that kid doing? The one who was riding the bike?"

"I'm sure he's okay."

"Did he have to stay in the hospital?"

"I don't think so."

"Can you find out for me? I need to know."

"I'll see what I can do."

He obviously cared about the kid. After all, he'd avoided the children and had chosen to slam into the semi instead. And his follow-up interest in the boy was touching.

She couldn't help thinking of him as a hero, the reckless and rebellious sort, like Han Solo in the first set of *Star Wars* movies.

So what made this guy tick?

She walked around the bed and opened the blinds, only to get an immediate complaint.

"Hey, what are you doing? Trying to kill me? The glare hurts my head."

"Sorry."

"They were closed for a reason."

She twisted the control rod, darkening the room again. "Do you need something for pain? I'll check the chart, and if it's time for more, I'll bring it in."

"I don't want whatever they've been shooting into my IV. It's messing with my mind. I hear people talking around my bed, but when I look, there's no one there. So I'd rather suck it up."

A tough guy, she thought, rebellious and surly, but with a tender heart. "There's other medication we can give you that isn't as strong. So there's no need for you to suffer."

"Right now I'd feel better if I could just sleep it off."

With the extent of his injuries and the seriousness of the concussion, she didn't think he'd wake up feeling any better. "All right, I'll leave you alone for a while so you can go back to sleep. I'll come in to check on you later."

She glanced at his monitor, noting the numbers were within normal range, and checked his IV drip. Everything was as it should be, so she headed for the door. But before leaving his room, she took one last look at her patient.

And for the second time in minutes, she wondered who the real Chase Mayfield was.

Shaking off her curiosity, she stepped out the door and returned to the third-floor nurses' desk, where Dr. Nielson sat, jotting down notes in a patient's chart.

Just last year, when Betsy took over Doc Graham's practice in Brighton Valley, Molly had been the first nurse she'd hired. They'd worked together only one day before the two became friends.

"How's Mr. Mayfield doing?" Betsy asked.

"He's complaining about the effects of the Demerol. Can we switch him to something else?"

"Sure, if that's what he wants. I'll write up an order for some Vicodin."

"By the way," Molly said, "he was wondering about the boy's condition. I didn't stick around the E.R. last night to find out, but I suspected that he'd been treated and released."

"Tommy Haines? Yes, he broke his wrist and knocked the growth plate out of whack, so I called in Dr. Jessup from orthopedics."

"Other than that, I take it there weren't any other complications and he went home?"

"No, that was it." Betsy closed the chart she'd been

working on and turned to Molly. "No other *physical* complications."

"What do you mean?"

"His mother is struggling just to pay the rent and to put food on the table, so she hasn't been able to keep up on the medical insurance premiums for him and his younger sister. That's why she declined riding in the ambulance. She didn't want to get hit with another bill she couldn't pay."

So there was another cost for Brighton Valley Medical Center to absorb, Molly thought. Not that it was a biggie, but every dollar added up.

BVMC was a new hospital that had had its grand opening a year or so ago. In a sense, it was up and running and doing very well. But it was struggling to stay afloat financially in a community that couldn't quite support a medical facility at the present. However, if the population continued to grow as the investors hoped it would, the hospital would be in much better financial shape next year.

"I'll contribute toward the boy's medical bill," Molly said.

"Again?" Betsy leaned a hip against the nurses' desk and crossed her arms. "You can't keep paying toward every indigent case we get."

"I know. But I've got the money, and it makes me feel good to help. Besides, BVMC doesn't need to drop further into the red. I'm just looking out for my job and my livelihood."

"There's got to be a better investment for your money," Betsy said. "Like a new car or that vacation you've never taken."

Maybe so, but Molly lived a simple life; it was just her and her cat, Rusty, at home, so her savings account was healthy. In addition, there'd been a major insurance settlement following the accident that most people didn't know about. She'd used a portion of it for college, but she hadn't touched the rest.

Randy Westlake, the last guy she'd dated, had known about the money, although he hadn't known exactly how much.

"You need to buy a house," he'd told her time and again. But it had bothered her that he was a real estate agent and stood to benefit if he was able to talk her into a purchase.

"Why throw your money away on rent?" he'd asked her. "There are a lot of nice houses near your grandmother's rest home that are much roomier and a lot nicer."

Yes, but none of them were as centrally located to all the places Molly frequented, like BVMC, the market and Rose Manor Convalescent Hospital.

No, the one-bedroom house she rented was perfect for her.

Randy had brought up the move and the money one time too many, and they'd finally parted ways. But not before he accused her of suffering from survivor's guilt and hoarding the "blood money" she'd received from the insurance settlement.

The accusation had been a low blow, lancing her to the quick, but only because she'd expected him to understand. She'd put the past behind her, whether he believed that or not, and she was content with her life and the place in which she'd chosen to live.

Besides, she had a new family now, the BVMC staff

and her patients. And while there was a part of her that yearned for a real home and loved ones, deep inside she feared getting too close to anyone again. It was tough enough when a patient died or a coworker retired or moved on for one reason or another.

So why get any more involved than that? Life was fragile, and loved ones could be taken away in a blink of an eye. That knowledge made her good at her job.

Of course, it also made for more than a few long and lonely nights.

At 2:14, Molly's pager went off while she was checking the dosage on Dr. Cheney's order for Carla Perez, the patient in 309. She glanced at the display and saw that Chase was calling her. She'd go to him just as soon as she gave the meds to Mrs. Perez, who'd had an appendectomy yesterday and was complaining of pain.

It didn't take her very long to stop off in 309, but by the time she entered Chase's room, she found him climbing out of bed.

"Where are you going?" she asked.

"To the bathroom."

As he got to a wobbly stand, the edges of his hospital gown split apart, as they were prone to do, revealing his backside and a nicely shaped butt.

She studied the appealing vision just a tad too long before asking, "Do you need some help?"

"I'll be okay." He reached for the IV pole, using it to steady himself, then shuffled to the bathroom.

She followed a few steps behind him, her gaze still drawn to his butt.

Not bad, she thought, not bad at all.

She wasn't in the habit of ogling her male patients, so the fact that she'd done so with this one didn't sit very well with her. As he slipped into the bathroom, leaving the door ajar, she stood just a couple of feet away, prepared to act if she had to.

He took care of what he went in to do, then the water in the sink turned on. Moments later, after the faucet shut off, he uttered, "Oh, damn."

She pulled open the door, only to find him about to collapse on the floor. She wrapped her arms around his waist, trying her best to support him.

"Wouldn't you know it?" he said, teeth clenched in a grimace of pain. "I've got a pretty nurse in my arms, and look at me. I can't even make an improper move, let alone a proper one."

"Cute," she said, wresting a hand free just long enough to push the call button on the wall. The man was a lot bigger and heavier than she'd realized.

"Why do I have to be laid up when an opportunity like this arises?"

While she held him, she tried to lower the lid of the commode so she could make a place for him to sit.

"Next time you need to get up," she said, "call me, okay?"

"Good idea. Maybe then I'll be stronger and better able to enjoy your tender loving care."

About the time Molly managed to sit Chase on the commode, Evie Richards, a nurses' aide, came in. "Need some help in here?"

"Yes. As soon as he catches his breath, we need to get him back to bed."

"Two pretty nurses taking me to bed," Chase said. "And I'm just about down for the count. What a shame."

If Evie had been young and shapely, rather than middle-aged and a bit on the plump side, Molly might have considered Chase to be more of an obnoxious player than a charming flirt.

Of course, given the chance, and away from a hospital setting, he might be both.

She supposed time—and some healing—would tell.

Once he was back in bed, Evie left the room. But before Molly could follow her out, Chase asked, "Did you ever find out anything about how that kid is doing?"

"He broke his wrist. His mom took him home last night."

"Good. I'm glad he's going to be okay."

"I hope so," Molly said, thinking about the single mom's plight.

"What do you mean by that?" Chase asked.

"Well, there's some financial difficulties—" Molly tucked a strand of hair behind her ear. "I'm sorry. I shouldn't have said anything."

He seemed to ponder her words, his brow knit together.

For a moment, she again tried to imagine the handsome man reflected in the picture on his driver's license, rather than the guy with a battered face.

"What kind of financial difficulties?" he asked.

"He lives with his mom and a sister, so there's just one income. And no medical insurance."

Oops. What had gotten into her? She stopped herself

from saying anything more. It was just that he seemed so sympathetic—and genuine—that the words had tumbled out before she knew it.

"Do you have a name and address for them?" he asked.

"Even if I did, I couldn't give it to you."

"But the hospital must have it."

"I'm sure they do, but they won't give out that information. And I shouldn't have told you what I did."

"Even if I wanted to pay the medical bill for them?"

"That's really nice of you," she said. "But I heard someone else has already offered to pay for it."

"I'm going to do it," he said, his voice sounding more certain—and a lot healthier—than it had since he'd arrived at the hospital.

She suspected that people didn't tell him *no* very often, and that he didn't like it when they did.

"Can you please let the billing department know?"

Molly supposed she could. If Chase took care of the Haines' bill, there were bound to be new ones that she could pick up. Not that she planned to pay for any and all outstanding accounts, but the ones involving kids or others that tugged on her heartstrings were another story. "All right, I'll tell them."

"Get me a number," he said. "And I'll cut the hospital a check."

Apparently Chase Mayfield was much more than a pretty face—and a nice butt. A whole lot more. And Molly found herself even more intrigued by him.

The charming race car driver was enough to make a woman forget she was a nurse. Almost. But Molly would never forget. It was too much a part of who she was.

"I'll see what I can do," she said, trying her best to rein in her wayward thoughts.

Then she turned and walked away, leaving him to watch her go.

As Chase lay stretched out on the bed, his personal Florence Nightingale disappeared into the hall. When he was sure she was gone and out of earshot, he picked up the telephone, pushed nine for an outside line and called his parents' house in Garnerville, Texas. His eyesight, which was still limited, and his fingers, stiff and sore from the accident, weren't cooperative, so he had to dial the number several times before he got it right.

His mother answered on the third ring. "Hello?"

"Hey, Mom. It's Chase. What are you doing?"

"The girls and I were just sitting at the kitchen table, drinking iced tea and planning a surprise party for your father's sixtieth birthday."

The girls in question were obviously her daughters-in-law, the wives of his older brothers.

"It's on a Saturday this year," his mother added, "so I hope you'll put it on your calendar before you get it all filled up. Your dad would be so disappointed if you missed it again, especially with it being such a biggie."

"I'll be there," Chase said, even if he didn't have a calendar handy. "Tell Callie, Susan and Jana hello for me."

"I will."

"Have you got a minute?" he asked.

"For my baby? I've always got time for you, Chase."

He supposed she always managed to find it, but when he'd been younger, he'd often felt as though he was in the way, as if his birth had somehow thrown the family dynamics out of whack.

His parents had never come out and said it, but his brothers had. And he'd sensed it often enough.

He always carried a credit card or two with him, so he could use one to pay the hospital for the kid, as well as any charges that might be left to pay for himself, but that would put his name out there, plus the statements went directly to Gerald Barden, who'd been watching them closely. And he wasn't ready for the questions Gerald would have.

"What do you want me to do?" she asked.

"I'm out of the area right now, so I'm going to need someone to be my right hand. And I hoped you'd do it for me."

"Sure. Does it need to be done today?"

He wanted to say yes, but he hated to be demanding. "No, tomorrow is fine. Since you have a spare key to my place, I'd like you to go inside and get my checkbook out of the desk drawer in the den. And I'd like you to mail it to me."

"Let me get a pen and paper to write down your address."

Uh-oh. All of a sudden, something he'd thought would be easy to orchestrate when he picked up the phone suddenly seemed a bit more complicated than he'd expected. And a fuzzy brain wasn't helping.

What address did he give her? The hospital's? No, he knew his mother, and she'd be here before he could blink an eye.

"You know," he said, "I just realized that I don't have

the address in front of me. I'll give you a call with it later, okay?"

"All right, but why do you need your checkbook?"

"I found out about a family that's struggling financially, and I'd like to give them some money."

"That's really sweet, Chase. I'm proud of you."

He hadn't been trying to impress his mother, but he couldn't help being glad that he had. And the fact that his act had touched her was also a sign that his plan would work.

If his sponsors got wind of what he was doing, and if the newspapers did, too…well, let's just say that he could use some good press for a change.

Not that he minded helping the family out. But to be honest, his motive hadn't been entirely altruistic. The good PR was an added benefit.

"Where are you?" his mom asked.

"I'm…" He glanced at the hospital room, knowing he'd have to be clever. He might have given his poor mother a few headaches while growing up, but he'd never lied to her and didn't want to start now, especially when his senses weren't as sharp as usual. "I guess you could say I'm taking a break from the rat race and kicking back."

"You have no idea how happy I am to hear that. I worry about you not getting enough sleep, Chase. The newspapers and magazines make it sound as though you've been keeping some late nights."

"Not recently," he said. He was going to fly under the radar for a while, just as Gerald Barden had ordered.

"That's a relief."

Maybe so, but settling down wasn't going to be permanent—but he wouldn't tell her that.

"Who's there with you?" she asked. "A woman? A girlfriend, maybe? If you were serious about someone, you'd tell me, wouldn't you?"

His mom would be the first to know. Everyone else in the Mayfield family was happily married, and when he and Pamela had divorced, he'd felt as if he was the only failure on the family tree.

He was just about to tell her he was alone and that there wasn't a woman in his life that he'd consider significant when his Florence Nightingale returned to his room. And when she did, some of the pain- and drug-induced fog in his brain lifted.

If word got out that he had a girlfriend, maybe then the gossip that bordered on truth would die down, and then Barden and the others would lay off him for a while.

Of course, Chase didn't actually need to *have* a girlfriend; rumors of a special lady in his life might be all that was needed.

A smile broke out, which forced the Vicodin-dulled ache in his head to return and caused him to relax his facial muscles. "Actually, that's exactly what I'm doing, Mom. I'm with a pretty blonde named Molly, and she just walked back into the room."

The nurse halted, and her lips parted as Chase decided to toss out information his mother could blow out of proportion. In fact, he was going to enjoy watching Nurse Molly's reaction to his words.

"You'd really like Molly, Mom. She's been giving me some long-needed TLC."

Molly crossed her arms, shifted her weight to one hip and lifted her brows in an I-can't-believe-you're-doing-this way.

Her expressive blue eyes sparked with both amusement and disbelief, making her prettier than ever. And he couldn't tear his gaze away from her.

Even in a pair of pale blue hospital scrubs, she promised to be shapely underneath.

For a moment the girlfriend rumor didn't sound the least bit far-fetched.

When his mom mentioned the party again and suggested he bring Molly, Chase said, "You bet. I'll tell her all about Dad's birthday at the end of next month. Of course, she may get tired of me by them, boot me out of her life and tell me to find another bed to warm."

"Now, you be nice to her," his mom said. "And stop teasing her like that. I know you, and she must be listening, no doubt embarrassed. But if you really were sleeping with her, you wouldn't be talking about it, especially with me. So she must be holding out. And if so, good for *her.* She's got morals and brains. I like her already."

Chase laughed, but only until the pain shot through his head again. "Hey, Mom, I'll have to give you a call later with that address, okay?"

"Sure. But if you want it to arrive tomorrow, you need to get it to me before the post office closes. And be sure to say hello to Molly. Tell her that I hope to meet her soon."

"I will."

The call ended, and Chase fumbled with the phone as he tried to hang up.

"What was that all about?" Molly asked.

"My mother said to give you her best."

"You told her you were on vacation? With a blonde named Molly?"

"Actually, 'vacationing' was her idea. I said I was kicking back."

"Oh. So you're one of *those*." Her eyes sparked again, and her tone suggested she hadn't meant it as a compliment.

His smile faded, but this time it wasn't just to make his head and face feel better. "I'm one of what?"

"A creative liar. A guy who knows how to fabricate an alibi or an excuse without actually coming right out and perjuring himself."

"No, I'm usually pretty up-front and honest, even with the ladies I date. But in this case, I didn't want to worry my mother. So I'm just…creating a myth that will put her heart at ease."

But for some reason, the thought of kicking back with Nurse Molly in his bed was making him feel better than any pain meds had.

## *Chapter Three*

It had been a long, grueling day, and by the time Molly stopped at the market to pick up a bag of cat litter, a quart of milk and a dozen eggs, it was well after nine.

She had grocery shopping down to a science, though. As long as she could pack it all in a single bag, she could carry it on her bike.

After removing her helmet and leaving her bicycle on the front porch, she unlocked the door and entered the living room, where she'd left a lamp on earlier so she wouldn't return to a dark house.

Rusty, who'd curled up on the recliner, meowed out a welcome, then yawned.

"You're in luck," she told the orange tabby. "The Brighton Valley Market carries your favorite kitty food again."

She kicked off her shoes, made her way to the recliner and gave Rusty's head an affectionate scratch. "How was your day?"

Rusty leaned into her hand to allow for a better massage and meowed his response.

"Yeah," she said, "mine, too. Long and tiring."

But it had been interesting, as well. And having Chase Mayfield as a patient had made it even more so.

Molly walked into the kitchen, with its pale yellow walls and white café-style curtains over the sink. She set the cloth grocery bag on the ceramic tile counter and put away her purchases. Then she fixed herself a micro-waveable dinner, which she stocked in the freezer for nights when she didn't feel like cooking.

Instead of sitting down at the table to eat, she carried her meal into the bedroom, where she kept her computer.

As the screen lit up, she logged on to the Internet and did a Google search on Chase Mayfield. She was only doing it because of professional curiosity, she told herself. As a way of getting to know her patient better.

But at the same time, she couldn't deny more than a tinge of feminine interest.

Sure enough, she found page after page of refer-ences—to his Web site, to newspaper articles, to lists of racing wins and awards.

She spent the next several hours reading up on her famous patient, starting with the virtual press kit on his site which claimed he was a skilled driver with a win-ning personality. But as she went on, she found solid evidence that he enjoyed the nightlife, Texas A-list parties and beautiful women.

Somewhere in the midst of her search, she learned that he'd married Pamela Barden, the daughter of his primary sponsor.

The two had looked good together in photos, although Pamela, with her dark hair hanging long and straight, appeared to be more plain and nondescript than her handsome husband. The more Molly read, the more it seemed that Pamela preferred a simpler life, one of charity work and philanthropy, while Chase seemed to blossom in the limelight.

Apparently the couple had divorced a year or so ago. Molly, who'd already drawn her own conclusions, wasn't surprised to hear that.

Had Chase fallen to temptation on the road? Had he cheated on Pamela? Dumped her for one of the leggy, voluptuous beauties that flocked around him these days?

There were certainly plenty of dots to connect, and Molly remembered Chase saying something about flying under the radar. What had he meant by *that?*

The more she read, the more questions she had—and the more intriguing he became.

Her interest didn't please her, though. Instead, it left her uneasy. She wasn't sure what unsettled her the most, his dangerous career or his flashy, high-profile life.

Either way, she had to get over that silly little…what? That little crush she'd developed?

No, it definitely wasn't that.

She just found him interesting, that's all. And God only knew why she did.

Chase Mayfield would be the worst person in the

world for her to get involved with. And she'd best keep that in mind when she went back to work tomorrow.

The next morning, Molly kept busy with all of the patients she'd been assigned, so she wasn't able to check on Chase as often as she had the day before.

Well, that wasn't entirely true. She'd gone to see about him as often as necessary, but certainly not each time he'd crossed her mind.

And that was *so* not a good sign.

Neither was giving him her home address to use for his mother to mail him his checkbook, which he'd talked her into doing yesterday afternoon.

What had provoked her to agree to that? She was usually more guarded with her patients—and with most people, for that matter. But her sympathetic nature had run away with her.

Or had it been more than that?

Chase Mayfield, she had to admit, was a charming rogue who could be very persuasive.

During her lunch break she'd ridden her bike home, taking the side streets as usual. And sure enough, she'd found a package for Chase in her mailbox. She'd given it to him when she got back to the hospital.

"Thanks," he'd said, taking it from her and opening it. "You're the best, Nurse Molly."

Was she?

His praise had made her smile, yet it left her a little uneasy, too.

She'd watched as he'd filled out the amount, then

scratched out his signature. She'd wondered what a handwriting expert would have to say about the man who made such big, bold strokes.

While she waited for him to finish, she'd felt like an autograph-seeking groupie. So once she had the check in hand, she'd lifted it and fanned it in the air. "I'll get this to the billing department."

"Thanks, but before you go, I have a question for you. Where've you been hiding out? I've missed you."

Had he? Or had he been playing with her? She feared that with Chase it would be hard to know which.

"I was letting you sleep so you can recover faster," she told him. "I'm sure you're eager to be discharged so you can get out of here."

"Yeah, but there are a few perks." His face was still battered, his eyes puffy and bruised, but he had a nice smile. A flirtatious smile.

Had he meant her?

Oh, for Pete's sake, she scolded herself yet again for giving him and his playful comments so much thought.

Chase was a charmer, that's all. And she was a fool for considering him to be anything else.

Molly went back to work, although her thoughts continued to drift back to Chase whenever there was a lull on the floor.

As the afternoon wore into evening and the sun dipped low on the Texas horizon, she sat at the nurses' desk, keeping busy—and away from Chase's bedside. Things were pretty quiet and peaceful on the floor now, which was good.

At the sound of shoes clicking on the tile floor, she

looked up to see Betsy approaching the desk. The dedicated physician didn't smile as much these days as she had when Molly first met her, but she appeared to be even more solemn than usual.

"Is something wrong?" Molly asked.

"No, not really. I just got back from a visit with Tommy Haines and his mother, Diana. I told them I was checking on his cast, but I'd also wanted to let Diana know that the medical bill had been paid. The other night, she seemed to be really stressing about it, and since they can't afford a phone, the only way to do that was to stop by and tell her in person."

"That was nice of you."

"I suppose, but it nearly broke my heart to see the way they were living."

"It was that bad?"

"Well, the kids were clean and happy, but their clothing was tattered from wear and too small for them. And when Tommy's sister opened up the pantry in search of a snack, the shelves were pretty bare."

It wasn't unusual for the hospital staff to come into contact with poor families. They always had a list of social service agencies to which they could refer them. They couldn't get personally involved with every case, but apparently, this particular situation had touched Betsy in a way some of the others hadn't.

"I wish I had more to give them than the news that they didn't owe money for Tommy's bill," Betsy said. "I gave Diana a hundred dollars, which she didn't want to take. I had to insist that she spend it on the kids. But I have a feeling it isn't going to stretch very far."

From what Betsy had said in the past, and Molly had gathered, Betsy had some money from a trust fund her aunt had left her, and as a successful doctor, she'd managed to save quite a bit over the years. But those funds were no longer available to her.

Most people didn't know it, but Betsy was one of the investors in BVMC. And while she certainly wasn't one of the principals, she'd put the bulk of her money into the hospital investment.

Thank goodness she had. Otherwise her ex-husband would have cleaned her out completely before he'd disappeared six months ago, leaving her with a slew of bills to pay and an empty bank account.

Of course, that was another tidbit that most people didn't know.

"On top of the financial troubles," Betsy added, "Diana is taking care of her elderly grandfather, who's clearly showing signs of dementia. He used to babysit for her so she could work part-time at the fabric store, but he's at a stage where he needs almost as much care as the children do."

"That's too bad," Molly said. "Has she considered putting him in a convalescent hospital?"

"Yes, but the man raised her, and she feels an obligation to keep him at home as long as she can."

Molly could relate to that. She'd had to deal with her own grandfather's health issues—not dementia, but a stroke. "Diana is in a tough spot."

"I know." Betsy blew out a weary sigh. "I gave her the contact number for a social worker who is a friend of mine, but I still felt…ineffective."

Molly wasn't sure how much help she could be, but she'd like to do something, especially since Chase had picked up the cost of the medical bill. "Would you mind giving me their address? Maybe I can take them something myself."

"It's a long ride on a bicycle," Betsy said, "even for you. You'd have to take your car."

Betsy was one of the few people at the hospital who knew that Molly preferred not to drive when she didn't have to. Not that it was a big secret; she just didn't think it was anyone's business but her own.

"Do Diana and the kids live in Brighton Valley?" she asked Betsy.

"Yes, but it's on the opposite side of town. They live in a trailer park on Sage Brush Trail."

Molly was torn between the sympathy that urged her to visit Diana Haines and the discomfort she felt whenever she slid behind the wheel. But there was only one way to get to the other side of town, and that was by car.

She could call a cab, but she made a lousy passenger—white knuckles and the whole nine yards. She felt powerless in the backseat, not to mention vulnerable, so she rarely kept her mouth shut, no matter who she rode with.

In retrospect—and with a nursing degree now under her belt—she realized that she probably should have had some counseling right after the accident.

Her grandparents had lost their only child in that accident, and seeing their eyes well with tears each time they thought of her father had made her own grief nearly unbearable. They'd been so caught up in their pain, they hadn't realized how tough it had been for her, although that's probably because she masked it so well.

But why make any of them suffer any more than they had to?

"Do you have a space number for the Haines?" Molly asked.

"Yes, it's two-twenty-three. It's close to the entrance, so you shouldn't have any trouble finding it."

No, her biggest problem would be in mustering her courage for the trek.

As long as she knew exactly where she was going, she did okay driving into Wexler or even to Evansville, which was ten miles to the east. But whenever she had to drive anywhere unfamiliar, she got a little uneasy.

But, hey. It wasn't that bad. She would just put on her seat belt, adjust her mirrors, stay under the speed limit and keep lots of space between her car and the other vehicles on the road.

So what if she had to deal with a few impatient drivers who honked at her?

"I'll probably stop by sometime tomorrow," she said, thinking it would be best if she had more daylight hours ahead of her and she didn't have to risk being on the street at night.

"Thanks, Molly." Betsy smiled, but before she could add anything else, her pager went off. "Uh-oh. That's my answering service. I've got to call in."

Molly nodded, just as her pager went off, too. She glanced at her own display screen. Room 310.

Chase needed her.

* * *

Chase lay in bed, his television on the blink. He supposed he could have used the call button, which would have paged any nurse at the desk, but it wasn't just any nurse he wanted to see; it was Molly.

Why did he get the feeling she was avoiding him today?

Had he gone too far when he'd asked her to let him use her mailing address?

No, it couldn't be that. She wouldn't have given it to him if she hadn't wanted him to know it, at least subconsciously.

And if that was the case, she wouldn't be disappointed that she had. After giving it to his mother, he hadn't disregarded it. Instead, he'd memorized it, and once he got out of here, he'd send her flowers. Or maybe he'd even stop by for a surprise visit. He wondered what she was like away from the hospital.

"Did you need something?" Molly asked from the doorway.

"Yeah. My television isn't working."

She walked over to the wall-mounted TV, clicked a button and turned a dial. The screen kicked right on. "It looks okay to me."

"Sorry about that." He glanced at his remote control, wondering why it hadn't worked for him.

"They get a bit temperamental sometimes," she said.

As she started for the door, he asked, "Do you have a minute?"

"Sure, why?" She returned to his bed.

"I don't know. I guess I've got a little cabin fever." He didn't want to admit to being lonely and bored. Or that he hadn't wanted to talk to just anyone, especially when the only one around here that piqued his interest was Molly.

She took a seat in the chair next to him. "How's your shoulder doing?"

He shrugged the side that didn't hurt. "They thought there was some nerve damage, so they called in a specialist. But the orthopedic surgeon thinks that an old injury has flared up. He said something about physical therapy, but I'm not sure what he decided for sure. He wants to consult with the first doctor."

"Things are pretty cool here, but when the other doctor is called, news of your accident could get out."

"I guess that's okay." Now that he'd written that check for the boy's medical expenses, it wasn't as important to keep his identity a secret.

Originally, he hadn't wanted Gerald Barden and the other sponsors to find out that he'd ended up on the eleven o'clock news within an hour of their straighten-up-and-fly-right speech. But they'd undoubtedly like hearing that he'd stepped in and had done something noble, like paid a kid's medical bill.

So he asked, "Does the boy's mother know that the hospital has been paid?"

"Yes, Betsy—I mean, Dr. Nielson—went to tell her earlier today, although the situation was worse than we thought."

Chase hoped the boy hadn't been injured more seriously than he'd originally been told. "What do you mean?"

"I'm sorry," Molly said, reading the fear in his eyes. "I wasn't talking about his broken wrist. The family's financial situation isn't very good. And on top of that, his mother is also trying to care for her grandfather, who has dementia. She'd like to get a job, but she doesn't have anyone to care for the kids. The old man used to babysit for her, but now she's afraid to leave him unattended, so her job prospects are more limited than ever."

Damn, the poor woman had it rough. And while his paying that medical bill had undoubtedly helped her, Chase figured it would take a whole lot more than that to make her life easier.

"Where does she live?" he asked.

"In a trailer park on the other side of town."

Chase's memory of the night of the accident was a bit fuzzy, but he had been driving in a neighborhood. He remembered a paved road, a curb and gutter, trash cans along the side of the road—and not one single trailer or mobile home. They'd either been visiting someone or they'd wandered away from home. Either way, they should have been tucked in bed, not running in the street.

"What were those kids doing out so late the other night?" he asked.

"I'm not sure, other than looking for a cat that ran off. The little girl went after it, and then the boy went after her."

And they'd ended up in the middle of the street with a '63 Corvette barreling down one lane and a semi down the other.

"I'm going to visit them tomorrow during my lunch hour," Molly said.

"Why?" he asked.

She bit down on her bottom lip as though pondering her reason. Or was she holding back on sharing it with him?

He supposed it was only natural that a nurse would have a soft spot.

Finally, she said, "I'm not sure what I'm going to do, but I suspect I'll probably give them some money before I leave."

"Do you do that very often?" he asked. "Give money to people in need?"

"I live pretty simply, so I have extra. And if I can help ease someone's pain and suffering, then I do what I can." She looked at him, those big blue eyes zooming in on him, pressing him into the mattress, making him feel even more helpless than before.

"Don't look so surprised," she said. "You have a generous nature, too."

Not like that. Sure, he was glad he'd been able to help the family, but his primary motive hadn't been all that admirable. He wasn't about to admit it, though. Not when she was looking at him like he was some kind of hero and he knew he was anything but.

He hoped she wasn't too naive, that she didn't usually lay herself open to con men and others who would take advantage of her good-hearted nature. And he couldn't help thinking that she'd given him her address when she really knew very little about him. But that information wouldn't be used against her.

"By the way," he said, "I talked to my mother earlier today to let her know the checkbook had arrived, and she asked about you."

"Only because you led her to believe we were sleeping together."

Chase couldn't help smiling at the thought. "I never came out and said that."

"You didn't have to." She smiled, and the room seemed to light up. Then she shifted in the chair. "Tell me about her."

"Who? My mom?"

"Yes. I'm curious about the woman who raised you."

Was she wondering about him, too? He suspected she was, and her interest in his boyhood rustled something deep inside him, something that had lain dormant for a long time.

"Her name is Sandra Mayfield, but everyone calls her Sandy. She's a redhead—at least, she used to be. She's also a great cook, when she doesn't have a grandkid tugging at her and wanting to play. What else do you want to know?"

"She sounds like a nice lady. Are you two very close?"

"Yeah, I guess you could say that. Why?"

"No reason."

Chase hadn't lived nearly thirty years without coming to the conclusion that there was always a reason behind a woman's question.

Molly checked her pager as though making sure it was on and that she wouldn't miss a call, but she remained seated.

"My mom used to be a champion barrel racer," he added. "And my dad was a bull rider. That's how they met."

"So your parents were competitive, too," she said. "That makes sense."

"You can say that again. I was the youngest in a family of four rough-and-tumble boys, each one vying to be top dog."

She smiled. "I imagine things were pretty rowdy at home."

"Not that any of us kids noticed, although I suspect my parents would disagree." He smiled, thinking back on the noise and the mess, while realizing his face didn't hurt so much anymore. "I learned early on how to stand alone, how to compete, how to fight for what I wanted."

He'd also learned to fight for what should have been rightfully his, although he wouldn't go into that with Molly.

"So you grew up around the rodeo?" she asked.

"Not really. We'd go to the ones that were held close to town, but my mom gave up barrel racing after she got pregnant with my oldest brother, and Dad threw in the towel after the next Mayfield boy came along."

"Was it tough for him to give it up?"

"I imagine so, but he never said. He had a family to support, and he wasn't bringing in all that much money as a bull rider."

"What does he do now?"

"He used to work on an oil rig," Chase said, "but he retired."

Actually, Phil Mayfield hadn't gone the gold-watch route. He'd been forced to stop working for health reasons, which had been tough on the man who'd prided himself on supporting his family over the years.

It had been even tougher for him to accept financial

help from one of his sons, though. But Chase was happy to do what he could, and as long as he kept his supporters happy and continued to race, it wasn't a problem paying the medical insurance premiums, the deductibles and the medication that wasn't covered by his dad's plan.

"What about your mom?" Molly asked.

"She's a housewife. There's not much to tell. They're good people—the salt of the earth, actually."

She wore an unreadable expression, the kind that was hard to decipher unless you really knew a woman. The kind that made him wish he knew Molly a whole lot better.

He wondered if she was on good terms with her parents, thinking that she might not be.

"Are you close to your family?" he asked.

"I was," she said. "I grew up in a happy, two-parent home in a small midwestern town. But when I was seventeen, my family died in an accident."

"I'm sorry to hear that." Chase had never lost anyone before, and he couldn't imagine losing them all in one fell swoop. "How did it happen?"

"A reckless driver blasted through a red light and broadsided the minivan we were riding in."

"I'm sorry," he said again, knowing the words were inadequate. "Were you hurt?"

"I got out with little more than a scratch." Her eyes clouded over—with grief, he suspected.

Or had it been more than that—an eerie sense of awe and disbelief?

Chase had once been involved in a collision with another driver, Darren Rydell. Chase had come out of it completely unscathed, but Darren had been so badly injured that he'd had to give up racing for nearly a year. When he came back, he'd lost the competitive edge he'd once had, while Chase, at least to some extent, had felt almost invincible. Like he had both skill and luck on his side.

"How did it happen?" he asked, wondering about the accident, about how she'd survived.

"My mom and dad had planned a trip to my grandparents' house in San Antonio. It was a Friday, and my dad had gotten off work early that day. He'd planned to leave home right after school let out, but there'd been a football game that night, and I was a cheerleader. It wasn't just any game. It was one with our crosstown rivals."

So the trip had been delayed, Chase realized.

"My mom suggested that I stay with a girlfriend that weekend, but I begged them to wait until after the game so I could go, too." She looked away, clearly shielding herself from his gaze.

"You're not blaming yourself for the accident, are you?"

"Not anymore. But sometimes I wonder what would have happened if they had left earlier in the day, if I'd been more agreeable about staying with a friend. Maybe they wouldn't have been in the wrong place at the wrong time."

Chase was a big believer in fate, which left little room for what-if questions. In his line of work, he couldn't worry about rabbits' feet or lucky charms. Otherwise, he'd be stressed and scared each time he accelerated or each time he went into a turn. "It wasn't your fault, Molly."

"You're probably right," she said, yet something told him she wasn't convinced.

"You were a teenager," he said. "A kid. Adults trump children all the time. But that time, your parents didn't. Don't blame yourself."

"It was twelve years ago, so I've done my share of stewing over it. But it's behind me now."

Maybe intellectually, he thought. But the way her shoulders drooped and the missing lilt in her voice told him that she hadn't been able to do so completely.

"I've had a few close calls, too," Chase admitted. "I don't even try to understand the ins and outs of them. Who knows why one person is born out of a million potential DNA combinations or why that same person dies before his or her time?"

She sighed. "I know you're right, but Jimmy, my brother, was just fourteen years old. He never even had a chance to live." She glanced at her pager again, and this time she got to her feet. "It just doesn't seem fair."

He reached out and grabbed her by the hand, giving her fingers a gentle squeeze. "I'm glad you wore a seat belt that night, Molly. And I'm glad you survived. Maybe God only needed three angels, and He knew that Earth could use a heck of a nurse."

"Maybe so," she said, offering him a smile that didn't quite reach her eyes. "I'd better get back to work, or the hospital might decide they need one less nurse."

Chase released her hand, then watched as she walked out of the room.

They had something in common, he decided. Molly couldn't quite understand why she'd been spared in that car accident.

And Chase, who'd been an unexpected, change-of-life baby in his family, had never been sure why he'd been born.

## *Chapter Four*

Molly couldn't believe she'd stayed in Chase's room for so long.

Or that she'd told him about the accident. She rarely talked about it anymore, even though it no longer haunted her as it had when the loss had been fresh, the pain so raw. But she still didn't like the fact that their conversation had stirred up memories of that dark and frightful night.

Of course, he seemed to stir up a lot of other things, too—like an attraction to her patient and a curiosity about him and the life he lived outside the hospital.

As she worked at the nurses' desk, she glanced up to see Colleen Bradley, one of the physical therapists on staff at BVMC, approach.

"Dr. Nielson asked me to stop by and see Mr.

Mayfield," Colleen said, "but she didn't tell me which room he's in."

Colleen, an attractive brunette in her early thirties, was tall, curvaceous and single, which had never seemed to matter before. But now, as Molly thought about her introducing herself to Chase, a twinge of something akin to jealousy sparked.

She'd come to enjoy the flirtatious conversations she'd had with Chase and didn't like the thought of him focusing his attention on anyone else.

Yet she had no claims on the man, and she was crazy to even consider taking their playful banter to heart.

So she managed a friendly grin and said, "He's in room three-ten."

"Thanks." Colleen returned a pretty smile, which only caused the green-eyed twinge to burrow in.

What was that all about? Molly had always liked Colleen, who was a professional and not in the habit of hitting on male patients.

But then again, neither was Molly.

Still, the uneasiness hounded her for the next ten—no, make that eleven and a half—minutes until Colleen finally exited Chase's room.

"I didn't know that Dr. Nielson had ordered PT for him," Molly said.

"She didn't. Mr. Mayfield is going to be discharged tomorrow, so she wanted me to give him some exercises to work on at home."

He was leaving tomorrow?

Molly knew it would be soon, but she hadn't expected...

Well, she wasn't quite ready…

The uneasiness built into a gnawing ache, although she couldn't figure out why. She'd been unhappy about having the race car driver assigned to her in the first place, and she'd been eager to see him go.

Yet now…?

She refused to give it any more thought. She'd just have to reel in any misplaced attraction for Chase Mayfield. No way could she risk losing her head over that man. She had a job to do, a career that not only meant the world to her, it had become her main purpose in life, a purpose that had arisen after the accident.

Jimmy, who'd not only been her younger brother but her closest friend, had lingered for almost two days before dying from his injuries, and Molly had stuck by his bedside until the end. She'd been too scared, too numb, at that point to be very aware of the hospital staff, although she'd known they'd been kind.

A year later, though, when Grandpa had been at Riverview Memorial following his heart attack, she'd been impressed with the compassion of the medical professionals who'd attended him. At that time, she'd begun to realize that she wanted to show that same kindness to others, to help them heal and get on with their lives.

The sound of the food cart rolling down the corridor drew her from her musing, and she glanced at the clock on the wall—6:03. The patients' dinners were right on time.

But rather than allow Amy Pederson to deliver all of the plates, Molly decided to pull out Chase's tray and take it to him herself.

"I was just heading to room three-ten," she said. "Why don't I take this one for you?"

For a moment, she pondered her reason for volunteering, but she quickly shook it off. It was probably best if she didn't think about her motive.

As she carried the tray into Chase's room, where he lay stretched out on the bed watching a ball game on TV, she said, "It's time to eat."

He turned down the volume, then brought the head of his mattress into a higher sitting position. "I hope you brought pizza and beer tonight. There's a game on."

"Oh, what a shame." She placed his meal on the tray table, then lifted the lid, revealing the food. "I think you're stuck with baked chicken, rice and green beans. But wait. There's tapioca pudding for dessert. Would you look at that?" She offered him a playful smile. "Yum! It sure looks good."

"Lucky me."

Instead of slipping away and returning to work, she hung out for a while, watching him poke at his food, noting that the swelling had gone way down in his face, that the bruises were fading. That he was beginning to look more and more like the photo on his driver's license each day.

The physical improvement meant he'd most likely be discharged soon, just like Colleen had said. And in spite of her initial uneasiness about being assigned to this particular patient, she wasn't at all happy to see him go.

She hated to admit it, but she enjoyed teasing him as much as he seemed to like teasing her. She supposed it was part of his fun-loving nature, but she didn't like the idea that he might have shared the same flirtatious banter with Colleen.

"How'd your meeting with the physical therapist go?" she asked, feigning indifference.

"Not bad. She worked with me a few minutes, then showed me some things I should do at home."

"Where's home?" Molly asked. She knew from her research, of course, but didn't want him to suspect she'd been seeking information about him on the Internet.

"Houston."

Molly nodded, acknowledging that she'd heard him, but she didn't leave. Instead, she remained in his room and watched him take a bite of chicken.

"Colleen said I was going to be discharged tomorrow," he said.

"She mentioned that to me, too, although I haven't talked to Dr. Nielson, and that will have to be her call." Either way, Molly realized, Chase would be leaving soon. And when he was gone, her workdays wouldn't be as enjoyable as they'd been since he'd been assigned to her.

"I'm going to have to find someone to get me some clothes to wear," he said. "Mine disappeared."

"We had to cut your clothing off when the paramedics brought you in." The night she'd undressed him, she thought, and at the memory, a smile stretched across her lips.

"What about my boots?" he asked.

"They should be in the closet here." She walked to the small wardrobe and opened the door. "Yes, they are."

"That's good to know." He tossed her a crooked grin. "I don't suppose you know someone who might pick me up a pair of jeans and a shirt? I'll make it worth his or her time."

Apparently, he didn't want to ask a friend or family member to do it for him. Instead, he was willing to pay someone to do it.

Normally, Molly didn't offer to do anything out of the ordinary for patients, but Chase was different from the rest. And there was also a shopping center a couple of blocks from her house and she wouldn't have to drive. "I'll do it as a favor, as long as I know what colors you like and what size you wear."

"Get me an extra-large shirt, and I'll trust you on the color. As far as the jeans go, I take a thirty-four in the waist and a thirty-two in length. And I'd prefer the boot cut, if you can find them."

"Consider it done." To be honest, she was actually looking forward to shopping for him. She'd pick up some underwear and socks, too.

It almost made her feel like a wife or a girlfriend, which was…interesting. She let the thought play out in her mind. Moments later, she said, "I'll bet you're looking forward to going home."

"Yes, but it wasn't so bad being here."

She wanted to think that his reason for saying that had something to do with her being his nurse, with the chats they'd had, but she couldn't allow herself to make that leap.

He'd probably been telling the truth when he'd told his mother that he was taking a break from the rat race. Maybe he'd wanted to hole up someplace where no one knew who he really was.

Where no one would bother him.

He hadn't had any visitors, so apparently he'd kept his whereabouts, as well as his identity, a secret.

Why had he wanted to?

He'd certainly had plenty of women in his life, and not one of them had come to see him. Did that mean he was unattached?

She knew it shouldn't matter to her. A guy like Chase probably liked playing the field. And if he didn't? Well, he wouldn't be interested in a quiet, stick-close-to-home nurse. And that was just as well. Molly had no business considering a relationship with a man who had a fast and reckless side.

"I'll bet there are a lot of people wondering where you are and what you're up to," she said.

"Probably. People try to second-guess me all the time, which is fine with me. I never have liked being predictable."

Unfortunately, Molly seemed to be far more curious than she ought to be. And she wasn't comfortable thinking she had so many questions about him and so few answers.

After all the paperwork had been completed, and Chase was officially discharged from the hospital, he waited for someone to take him outside.

When he'd tried to insist on walking, Dr. Nielson had said, "I'm sorry, Chase. Hospital regulations don't allow that."

So now here he was, wearing clothes Molly had bought him—black jeans and a light blue shirt—and waiting for someone to pick him up in a wheelchair and give him a ride outside.

"Are you ready to go?" Molly asked, as she rolled in the chair.

"Yeah." He took a seat, favoring his left knee, which the paramedics had thought he'd broken, but after X-rays, doctors had said no. "Are you my ride out of here?"

"Unless you'd rather have one of the orderlies do that."

"Nope. I doubt he'd be as pretty as you."

Her cheeks flushed, and he was glad that he'd put the color in them. He was going to miss her, he realized— a lot more than he'd expected.

"Who's going to pick you up?" she asked.

"I called a taxi."

She cocked her pretty head to the side, as though she found that odd. "Are you taking it all the way to Houston?"

"That's where I live."

"A two-hour cab ride is going to be expensive."

"Probably." But Chase wasn't going to ask anyone else to pick him up. There'd be too many questions, and now he wasn't exactly sure how he wanted news of his hospital experience and his generosity to unfold. When the story got out, he wanted to put his own spin on it, not someone else's.

As Molly took him down the elevator to the lobby, he said, "Did I ever tell you how much I hate being a passenger?"

"Yes, you did. And I can relate to that, since I feel the same way. I'd much rather be in control of the car, but sometimes it can't be helped."

After pressing the handicap button on the automatic door, she pushed the wheelchair outside and to the curb that was for loading and unloading passengers.

"I'm even less happy about riding with women drivers," he added, hoping to get a rise out of her. Damn, he was going to miss their banter, miss seeing her eyes light up when she dished it back to him.

"That's too bad," she said. "I could have left you in your room until one of the male orderlies was available."

"That's okay. At least you didn't take any wild turns or apply lipstick while you were in control."

"I'd never do that, especially in a car. When I'm driving, I'm very careful—hands on the wheel, eyes on the road. I don't even listen to the radio."

"If you ask me, that sounds a little too careful."

"I don't take chances, although I'm sure you do."

Not if he wasn't confident of his ability. "I'm not reckless, if that's what you mean."

"I'm glad to hear it."

The cab had yet to arrive, so they continued to wait curbside.

"How did you come to drive race cars?" she asked. "It would seem to me that if your family liked rodeos, that you would have chosen to be a bronc rider or that sort of thing."

"For what it's worth, I'm a pretty good cowboy." He stretched out his left leg and rubbed the top of his knee, which still hurt. "But after my dad gave up the rodeo, he started hanging out at the stock car races. Eventually, Dan Holbrook, one of the drivers, asked him to work in the pit. So I guess you could say that my brothers and I pretty much grew up at the track."

"Your mom, too?"

"It didn't take long for her to become a fan."

"When did you start driving?"

"Dan never had any kids of his own, and he took a liking to me. One day he let me drive his car, and said I was a natural. He talked my dad into letting me compete in the youth circuit."

"I'll bet your dad is proud of you," Molly said.

"He claims he is." By racking up wins on the track, Chase had finally been able to do what he'd been attempting to do ever since he'd been a kid trying to make a place for himself in the family: he'd proved himself worthy of respect.

But making his sponsors proud had been important, too—especially Gerald Barden.

When Chase had married Pamela—Gerald's only child—the wealthy racing enthusiast had offered to buy a top-of-the-line stock car and round up some other sponsors, enabling Chase to finally make his mark in the racing world. It had also allowed him to pay for his dad's current medical needs and to tell his brothers he didn't need their help.

So in spite of what others might think, racing wasn't just a matter of fun and games on his part.

"Here it comes," Molly said, pointing toward the approaching taxi.

When it pulled to the curb, Chase got out of the wheelchair, wincing when he put his weight on that left knee. But rather than climbing into the backseat, he took a moment to turn and look at Molly, to study her face, to memorize the bluebonnet color of her eyes, the way a light scatter of freckles dusted her slightly turned-up nose.

He was happy to be coming home—and a little disappointed that he wouldn't see her on a day-to-day basis any longer.

"Say," he said, running the back of his knuckles along her cheek. "How about going out to dinner with me sometime? I could pick you up and drive you into the city. We could make a night of it."

"Not unless you let me drive," she said.

"I don't know about that," he said, chuckling.

She didn't respond, and he figured she was giving the whole date-a-patient idea some thought.

What would it hurt if they saw each other again on a social level and took a let's-see-how-it-works-out approach?

She still seemed to be thinking it over, which didn't happen very often. Most women jumped at the chance to date Chase. But he knew how to make things happen. And in this case, he'd just give her a little push by making a surprise visit to 162 Johnston Lane.

He couldn't help tossing her a playful smile. "I'll see you around, Nurse Molly."

Then he climbed into the back of the cab and closed the door.

"Where are we going?" the driver asked.

"To the Lone Oak trailer park. I heard it was on the outskirts of town."

"I know where it is."

As the driver pulled away from the curb, Chase glanced back at Molly, who hadn't moved. She continued to stand at the curb, holding the back handles of the wheelchair and watching him go.

Chase knew when a woman was attracted to him.

And when it came to Nurse Molly, he fully intended to do something about it.

The Lone Oak trailer park, which was on the outskirts of Brighton Valley, was little more than a mobile home graveyard—at least, it seemed that way to Chase.

"This is it," the cabdriver said. "You want me to wait?"

"Yeah." Chase whipped out a ten-dollar bill. "I'll just be five minutes or so."

"Excuse me for asking," the guy said, "but what happened to you? You look like someone beat the hell out of you."

Chase had forgotten about that. He'd hate to scare one of the kids. He craned his neck to take a peek in the cab's rearview mirror, and while his eyes were both open, they bore shiners. And the scar across his brow looked a bit nasty and piratelike.

So now what?

Hell, he could always play it by ear.

"Wait here," he told the cabbie, not deigning to answer. "I'll be right back."

He wandered into the park, where he spotted two old men sitting in the shade provided by the dusty, red-and-white-striped awning of an old fifth wheel travel trailer. "Hey, guys. Do you know where I can find Diana Haines?"

He'd caught her name on the local news broadcast the day after the accident.

"Why do you want to know?" a slender, silver-haired man with a handlebar mustache asked.

"My name is Chase Mayfield. The other night, I was involved in a car accident down the street. Her kids saw it happen and called the paramedics."

"You the fellow who was driving what used to be a snazzy Corvette?" the heavyset man wearing red suspenders asked.

"That was me."

"You're not the race car driver, are you?" Slim asked.

"Actually, I am."

"No kidding?" The stocky fellow sat up straight, appearing to be impressed.

"I've got ID I can show you," Chase said.

Both men peered at him as though they were trying to look beyond the fading bruises on his face.

"I think he's telling the truth," Slim said. "And now it all makes sense. Clyde Crowley lives on Third Street, and he saw it all happen. But he didn't know who was involved, just that the sports car driver did some fancy steering and managed to avoid both kids."

Chase didn't respond. He just let them come to their own conclusions.

"What do you want with Diana?" Slim asked.

"I thought I'd stop by and check on the kids. I heard that she'd been having a tough time lately, and I wanted to see if there was something I could do to help her out."

"That's right nice of you," the heavyset man said, getting to his feet. "I can take you to her trailer."

"I'd appreciate it."

"My name is Howard Laughton," Slim said, leaning forward to stand up. "And this is Sudsy McClean."

"Sudsy?" Chase asked the heavyset man.

"I used to own a car wash," he said. "And that's a nickname some of my poker buddies gave me. Real name is Josh Douglas, but nobody calls me that anymore."

They headed down a graveled lane that stretched through rows of mobile homes, each one unique, until they came to a faded turquoise-and-white single-wide.

"This is it," Sudsy said. "The Haines place."

A beat-up old Chrysler was parked in the front, and a pair of Rollerblades lay on a small patch of dried-out lawn that needed to be mowed. Potted plants and a couple of pink geraniums lined the wooden steps to the front door.

Chase figured he'd be on his own from here on out, but both men hung back, waiting and watching. He wasn't sure if they remained out of curiosity or as protection for the single mom.

Either way, he didn't mind. They'd make the perfect witnesses and would put the right spin on the story, which would be yesterday's news in no time at all.

Sudsy and Slim—or rather, Howard—followed Chase up the steps and waited as he knocked on the door.

A small girl answered, her eyes wide as she studied Chase's injured face.

"Is your mommy home?" he asked.

The little girl nodded, but didn't move.

"Can you please get her?" he asked.

Again, she nodded. Then, after taking one last gander at him, she dashed off, calling her mother.

Moments later, Diana Haines, a petite brunette, came

to the door. She appeared to be concerned, leery. And Chase couldn't blame her.

"Yes?" she asked.

"Mrs. Haines, I'm Chase Mayfield, the guy who was in the accident the other night."

Her expression softened, making her appear almost attractive in a girl-next-door sort of way. "I'd wanted to talk to you. First of all, to apologize for my kids being out in the street. And secondly, to thank you for paying Tommy's medical bill."

"There's no need to apologize or thank me." Chase refrained from looking over his shoulder to make sure Sudsy and Howard had heard what she said. He knew they had.

"Come on in," she said. "I'm sorry about the mess."

"Don't be." Chase stepped into the small living room. "I grew up in a family with four boys. I know how kids are."

Diana continued to hold open the door, allowing the old men inside, too.

"How's Sam doing today?" Sudsy asked.

"He's all right."

Chase spotted a balding man in his late seventies seated in a black vinyl recliner, the newspaper spread out around him. He recognized the old men, and they both greeted him before returning their attention to Chase and Diana.

"How about Tommy?" Chase asked the mother. "How is he?"

"The broken wrist hurt him quite a bit for the first couple of days, but it's been a week now, and he seems to be feeling much better."

"And the cat?" Chase asked. "I'd heard it ran off and that they were looking for it."

"She…uh…" Diana scanned the small living area, noting the child who stood near a small television set with a rabbit-ears antenna. "She hasn't come home yet." Diana addressed her daughter. "Missy, would you please go get your brother?"

When the girl took off, Sudsy lowered his voice. "The coyotes are bad out here, and they were howling up a storm that night. None of us figure that cat's coming home."

Chase nodded. Maybe he ought to see what he could do about getting the kids a kitten as a replacement pet. He supposed he'd have to ask Diana first, though.

When a scruffy-haired boy entered the room, sporting a blue cast on his hand and forearm, Chase offered him a smile. "How are you doing, Tommy?"

"Okay."

"This is the man who crashed his car into that truck," his mother said. "The man who paid our medical bill."

"Thanks for not killing us," the boy said. "And for paying that bill. My mom was really worried about it."

Chase suspected she'd been worried about a lot of bills, and he was determined to do what he could to help. And, admittedly, it wasn't just because his generosity would help his own plight.

He thought of Molly, of her obvious concern for this family, and it made him feel connected to her—a part of something bigger than him. He pulled out his checkbook from his back hip pocket. Then he wrote Mrs. Haines a check for two thousand dollars.

And while he hoped the media got wind of what he'd just done, as well as Gerald Barden and his other sponsors, none of that seemed important right now.

The one person he really wanted to share it with was Nurse Molly.

## Chapter Five

"What in the hell happened to you?" Gerald Barden, who stood in the doorway of his sprawling ranch house as if his six-foot, two-inch frame had been rooted to the ground, gawked at Chase.

Apparently, he didn't intend to open the door wider, which was okay. Chase was eager to get home and lie down for a while, but he thought it was best if he talked to Gerald privately—and face-to-face. He was eager to set a few ground rules from his side of the negotiating table.

"What'd you do? Get in a bar fight with a gang of bikers?" Gerald, who was also Chase's former father-in-law, swore under his breath. "Apparently you didn't take that little chat we had seriously."

Actually, Chase had been giving that little chat a

whole lot of thought since he'd missed the turnoff and headed into Brighton Valley by mistake last week.

And the words had replayed over and over in his mind while he'd recovered in the hospital.

*We realize you're single and that women flock around you,* Gerald had said, as he gave a sweeping glance to the other men gathered in his study. *Lord knows we're not so old that we don't remember what it's like to have a little fun. But what we don't want to see is that kiss-my-ass attitude you've been displaying lately.*

Chase had wanted to blow off the wealthy businessmen, as well as their conservative values, but he couldn't afford to alienate any of them, especially Gerald, who'd clearly been the ringleader of the so-called meeting.

At that point, Gerald had settled his bulky frame into a tufted leather chair in his study and lifted his index finger in a move Chase had always found aggressive and threatening. *You're a hell of a driver, and we'd hate to lose you. But don't underestimate us.*

Chase would never underestimate Gerald, but he wouldn't be intimidated by him, either. And now that they were alone, it was best they got a few things straight.

"Damn," Gerald said, scrunching his nose as he studied Chase's battered face. "I hope those bikers got it worse than you did."

"Actually," Chase said, "I wasn't in a bar fight. I was in a car accident."

"Oh, yeah?" Gerald stepped aside, allowing Chase into the house.

"I'm not going to stay very long," Chase said. "The

cabdriver has the meter running, and I've got things to do at home."

"So what's this surprise visit all about?" the gentleman rancher asked, as he led Chase into his living room.

"I wanted to tell you that I didn't appreciate the way you laid out your agenda the other night."

"That chat we had wasn't personal," Gerald said. "You know that. If it had been, I would have cut you off as soon as I learned that you and Pamela had separated."

True. Most men might have severed all ties with a son-in-law the minute their only daughter had packed her bags, and Chase suspected Gerald had certainly given that idea a lot of thought. But in the end, he hadn't let family loyalty sway him, a decision that might have been influenced by the fact the divorce had been Pamela's idea—for the most part.

Needless to say, Chase had been upset about the split, but it wasn't because Pamela had broken his heart. At that point in their marriage, the relationship had become so strained, so distant, that he hadn't been surprised or torn up by his wife's announcement.

Instead, a daunting sense of failure had settled over him, something he'd found a whole lot harder to deal with.

Defeat had always gone against his grain, and what made matters worse, his entire family had a history of long and happy marriages. So telling his folks that he was getting a divorce had been one of the hardest things he'd ever had to do.

"Have a seat." Gerald indicated one of several chairs in the room.

"That's okay. I'll stand." Chase crossed his arms and

shifted his weight off his bum knee. "If you would have addressed my behavior privately, it wouldn't be an issue, Gerald. But I don't appreciate being called on the carpet in front of the other sponsors when a quiet heart-to-heart would have worked."

"It wasn't just my idea to call that meeting. Your behavior is a reflection on each of us, and I for one don't like the bad press." Gerald took a seat on the Italian leather sofa. "The others don't care for it, either. And neither does Pammy."

It still grated on Chase when Gerald referred to his daughter with the nickname he'd given her as a child. She was a college graduate, for Pete's sake. Besides, she'd cut all ties to Chase several years ago. "I'm not sure what Pamela has to do with this."

"Aw, hell, Chase. Everyone knows the two of you used to be married. And for that reason alone, it's a bad reflection on her."

Chase figured Gerald might be more concerned about the reflection it had on *him*—as an owner and a sponsor—but he couldn't be sure. "Pammy" always had been the apple of her daddy's eye, even though she'd been trying to break free of his influence for a long time.

If Chase truly believed his lifestyle was all that wild or was an embarrassment to Pamela, he might make a few changes. At least, he liked to think that he would. The two of them weren't exactly friends, but they didn't hold any animosity toward each other anymore.

In fact, last June she'd married a man whose family had a truckload of money and ran in the same circles as the Bardens. From what Chase had heard, she was happy now.

"I don't want to see Pammy or her in-laws embarrassed by anything you might do," her father added.

Now was probably a good time to mention the Haines family and his contribution, but instead, he kept that information close to the vest. Gerald seemed to think he had Chase all figured out, but he didn't.

No one did, and Chase liked it that way.

"I'll keep your words in mind," he told the man.

"You do that, son, because I'm as serious as a heart attack."

"I know you are. And so am I. You can say anything you want to me when we're in private, but I don't want an audience next time."

"All right. Fair enough." Gerald folded his arms over an ample belly. "You might consider settling down with one woman, though. That would certainly help."

"When I find the right woman, maybe I will." Chase nodded toward the doorway. "Now, if you don't mind, I need to head back to Houston."

As Gerald started to get to his feet, Chase stopped him. "Don't bother. I'll let myself out."

On his way to the front door, he stopped at a table near the entry, where a silver-framed picture of Pamela sat. He picked it up, taking time to reflect on the woman he'd once loved.

Chase had been twenty when he met Pamela at Texas A&M, and she'd been nineteen. Things had burned hot and bright at the start, and after a whirlwind courtship, they'd gotten married while still college students.

They'd spent a weekend-long honeymoon in Vail, then moved into a small apartment off campus, where they'd tried to balance the demands of school and a relationship. But it hadn't been easy, and about six months later, things had started going south.

They'd had some good times, some nice memories. But whatever affection and attraction they'd once shared hadn't been enough. The marriage hadn't been strong enough to weather life's storms—particularly all the time Chase spent away from home.

He'd told himself that he was committed to racing and the circuit, to the fame and glamour, but in truth, being a part of the stock car world had kept him too busy to face the truth: he didn't wholeheartedly love Pamela enough and had never felt completely accepted by the Barden family.

It had chapped his hide to learn that some people thought he'd only married Pamela for her money and her father's sponsorship. Anyone who truly knew Chase would tell you that he was no one's man but his own.

He'd chalked up the murmurs as being from jealous competitors who hadn't liked losing.

The truth was, Chase and Pamela had shared something special for a while, although it seemed to fizzle out nearly as quickly as it had heated up.

As time wore on, she found a man who was not only her social equal, but who had been ready to fully invest himself in a relationship.

Still, Chase had to admit that some people might find it unusual that Gerald had continued to sponsor his ex-son-in-law after the divorce. But Gerald was an avid racing fan and liked riding on Chase's coattails.

So life was good—or so Chase was prepared to argue.

But if he were being completely honest, he had to admit that true happiness had always eluded him—from the time he was a kid until now.

Maybe that's why he'd been going out so much at night and living life in the fast lane. Being home alone had never held much appeal.

Gerald seemed to think a steady relationship would provide Chase with better press. And maybe it would—for a while.

Chase knew quite a few groupies who would be thrilled to go out with him, but choosing just any woman wasn't going to work. He needed to find someone he wouldn't mind being officially paired with. Someone who would not only provide his sponsors peace of mind, but who would lend him a rock-solid sense of respectability.

As Pamela had done.

But that wouldn't work for very long. Chase might be able to play around and pretend that his life was exactly as he'd planned it, that he was happy being footloose and fancy-free. But he couldn't fake a romance, especially when he'd have to either get a woman to play along or lead her on unknowingly.

And Chase couldn't do that.

Besides, his marriage to Pamela had ended in disappointment. How could another relationship with someone like her fare any better?

Maybe he wasn't cut out to be solid and respectable. Maybe he wasn't meant to settle down.

He thought about his old man, who'd given up the rodeo to support his family and had never complained—

at least not that Chase was aware of. But the two of them were cut from different bolts of cloth.

A man like his father would have found a way to make his marriage to Pamela work. And he wouldn't have kowtowed to anyone, not even Gerald Barden— which led him back full circle.

The only woman who'd made Chase seem to be the least bit solid and family-oriented had been Pamela. And women like her were few and far between.

He replaced her picture frame on the polished oak credenza, then left the house. But on the way back to Houston, it wasn't Pamela's face he envisioned.

It was Molly's.


With Rusty curled up next to her, Molly sat on her sofa with a cup of herbal tea and read the newspaper, which she hadn't had a chance to look at earlier this morning. Instead, she'd cleaned the house and done the laundry. She'd also picked up groceries for the week.

Now, as the sun dropped low in the western sky, she turned to page B-1 again and looked at the black-and-white photo of the Haines family.

The wire services had finally gotten wind of Chase's accident and his hospital stay, as well as his generosity to Diana and the kids. The human-interest story had become big news within a week of his discharge.

So much for Chase wanting to keep his identity quiet.

Apparently, two gentlemen from the Lone Oak trailer park had learned what he'd done and had passed the word. Before long, the whole story was out, and the media had jumped on it.

According to this newspaper article, Chase had also extended an invitation to Diana and her kids to come to Houston for a preseason race.

Molly couldn't shake an indescribable ache whenever she thought about him, whenever she spotted his picture in the paper or heard his name on the news. He'd checked out of the hospital more than a week ago, and she still struggled with an unwelcome and lingering attraction to her patient, a man she should be glad that she'd steered clear of because of his wild and reckless lifestyle.

Of course, he hadn't seemed wild and reckless when she'd known him. And taking the single mother and her children under his wing was heartwarming. It also mocked the notion that he might have a selfish streak or an oversize ego.

She'd also read an article about his ex-wife this afternoon, but that was in the social section, which Molly usually didn't pay much attention to. Still, the name Pamela Barden-Jones had jumped out at her, and she couldn't help her interest in the charity auction Pamela had organized, a successful event that benefited an orphanage in Mexico.

Maybe philanthropy and generosity had been something both Pamela and Chase had in common when they'd been married.

The doorbell sounded, drawing her from her reading and her thoughts. She glanced at the clock on the cable television box, noting that it was well after five.

She padded to the door, wondering who could be stopping by. She spotted Chase on the front stoop, holding a bouquet of long-stemmed red roses and wearing a pair of black slacks, a soft blue button-down shirt and a dazzling smile.

Her heart flip-flopped, and her pulse skipped a beat. She wished she'd known he was coming, that she'd dressed with his visit in mind. She'd showered after cleaning the house, but she wasn't wearing anything out of the ordinary, just a pair of worn jeans and a pink cotton blouse.

"I brought these to thank you." He flashed her a crooked grin that only looked vaguely familiar, since the pink scar across his brow was the only sign of the facial injuries he'd suffered in the accident.

"You don't need to thank me. I was just doing my job." She held the doorknob with one hand and raked the other through the strands of her hair she hadn't taken time to style.

"But I wanted to get them for you. To thank you for letting me use your address and for shopping for me." He nodded at the door she was practically hiding behind. "Are you going to invite me in?"

Her mind, which had grown fuzzy and numb with the surprise of seeing him again, suddenly cleared, and she stepped aside. "I'm sorry. Yes, please come in."

He scanned the interior of her home, and she wondered how it measured up. The house was cozy, as far as she was concerned, and perfect for her and Rusty. But she supposed it might seem small and plain to a famous guy who was probably used to so much more.

"Nice place," he said.

She wanted to believe him, but found herself skeptical. With the money he had, he undoubtedly had a much bigger, much nicer house, but she thanked him just the same.

"Would you like some coffee?" she asked. "Or maybe some iced tea?"

"The tea sounds good. And if you don't mind, I'll take these into the kitchen for you so we can get them into some water."

She wasn't so sure that she wanted him to follow her through the house, but he seemed determined, and she was still trying to make sense of his visit and to regain control over the unexpected, heart-stirring situation. She felt almost naked without her scrubs and a hospital setting. Her job had become so much a part of who she was, and entertaining in her home was unusual.

Once in the doorway, she flipped on the light switch, then took the flowers from him. "Why don't you have a seat while I put these in water."

As he headed toward the nearest chair, she pulled out a vase from the cupboard under the sink and filled it with water. After clipping the end of each stem, she arranged the roses and carried them back to the table.

The vivid red flowers provided a shot of color to the small, functional kitchen, and so did the handsome man who was waiting for his tea.

"You look good," she said. Realizing that he might be reading something into her words, something she didn't want to reveal, she added, "I mean you look healed and back to normal."

"My knee is still a bit sore, but it's much better. I'm not favoring it too much anymore."

"Good." She pulled a glass from the cupboard,

added ice cubes from the freezer, then poured the tea from the glass jar that sat on the counter where she'd left it earlier.

"Sugar?" she asked.

"Just a little bit."

She fixed herself a glass, as well, then joined him at the table.

He took a sip of the tea, and she watched the muscles in his throat work as he swallowed. She found him even more intriguing than before, more attractive. And she wasn't quite sure what to make of it all.

"I'd like to take you to dinner tonight," he said. "There's a place in Houston that's one of my favorites."

No way did she want to make a two-hour drive, then have to return late at night. The roads were long and winding in places, and the chance of an accident or a breakdown increased after dark.

Yet she was drawn to Chase, and the thought of having dinner with him was far more appealing than it should be.

"We don't need to drive all the way to Houston," she said. "There's a nice little Italian restaurant just down the road a bit."

"All right, that sounds good to me. Do we need reservations?"

"Maybe. Unless we go early."

"I'm up for anything."

*Anything?* It seemed like such an open suggestion that her mind shot off in a zillion different directions, each one leading back to her house, to her bed.

And much to her chagrin, the thought of a romantic sleepover was far more appealing than it should be, probably because she'd gone without sex for so long.

Oh, for Pete's sake. It was just a simple dinner date.

Or was it? a small, inner voice asked. The roses suggested otherwise.

And so did a raging pulse on her part.

"I'll have to change clothes," she said.

"Go ahead. I'll just sit here and talk to your friend."

"My friend?"

He nodded low in the open doorway, where the orange tabby sat, checking out the only guest she'd invited in the house in months.

"His name is Rusty," she said. "He's a little slow warming up to people."

"I've got plenty of time," Chase said.

Meaning what?

Oh, for goodness' sake. She shouldn't be reading anything into his words.

"I'll just be a few minutes," she said, before heading to her bedroom.

Once inside, she opened her closet and started the tedious chore of deciding what to wear.

Maybe she should have suggested the pizza place on the corner instead of the much fancier Cara Mia's. It would have made choosing a proper outfit so much easier.

Or would she still be stressing about what clothes to wear?

"Darn it," she muttered.

She hadn't had a date in well over a year, and for

some crazy reason, she felt like Cinderella getting ready for the ball.

So where was a good fairy godmother when you needed one?

## Chapter Six

Cara Mia's was a fairly new restaurant with great food, an extensive wine list and Old World charm. It was also a short walk from Molly's house.

As she and Chase cut across the alley on their way to the mall, where the restaurant was tucked between the movie theater and a bookstore, the soles of their shoes—his boots and her black high heels—crunched on the graveled dirt.

"I've never walked to dinner before," he said, chuckling.

"When you live as close as I do to shops and stores, it's silly to jump into a car and drive." Of course, little did he know that she'd chosen the house in which she lived for that very reason.

Their arms brushed several times on the way to the

restaurant, and Molly felt the strongest compulsion to slip her hand in his. But while she'd always been determined to exercise as much control over her life as possible, she'd never been quite that bold.

Yet tonight was different, and her senses were reeling. She blamed it on the man sauntering next to her, on the woodsy scent of his aftershave, on his fame and the fact that any woman would be happy sharing an evening with him. So she reeled in her wild thoughts and managed to slow her rapid pulse rate.

This wasn't a date, and she'd better keep that in mind.

Within ten minutes of leaving her house, they reached the small, classy eatery that provided both patio and indoor dining.

"Do you mind if we eat outside?" he asked.

"No, that's fine." She didn't have a preference, although, as she scanned the dark-wood interior, the tables with candles flickering, the small bud vases with fresh flowers, she realized Cara Mia's was a lot more romantic than she'd remembered.

Or was that due to the man she was with?

She stole a look at Chase, saw his handsome profile, and her heartbeat kicked up a notch all over again.

The hostess, a young woman in her twenties, greeted them at the entrance, then escorted them to a linen-draped table on the patio that had been placed next to an outdoor heater and a pot of pink bougainvillea.

Chase pulled out a chair for Molly, and she took a seat. Then he sat across from her. The hostess handed them menus and a wine list, and a busboy brought them water spiked with lemon slices, as well as a basket of fresh-baked bread. Moments later, they were left alone.

From a hidden speaker, violin music played softly— something Italian and hauntingly romantic. With that added to the candle flickering on the table, she couldn't help feeling as though she was being wined and dined by the hero in a chick flick.

"You look beautiful tonight," Chase said, his blue eyes glimmering in the candlelight, his expression heart-stirring.

"Thank you." She tried not to let his words and his smile go to her head. In her rush to dress, she'd only done the best with what she had—hair, makeup and clothes.

After shuffling through the various outfits in her closet, she'd settled on a black dress she'd worn to a retirement party for one of the surgeons at Wexler General Hospital. She'd forgotten all about it until she'd spotted the dry cleaner's bag in a corner.

She'd purchased it more than two years ago, but it had a classic style and still fit as though it had been made with her body in mind.

"How about some wine?" Chase asked.

"That sounds good."

He motioned for the waiter, then asked her, "Red or white?"

"You choose. I'll be happy with either."

He ordered a bottle of merlot from a California winery, and before long, they'd both been served a glass. He lifted his in a toast. "Here's to getting to know each other outside the hospital."

"And away from the racetrack," she added, clicking her glass against his.

The resonant sound of crystal upon crystal rang out, adding to the magic of the evening. But Molly would be darned if she knew what to do, what to say. So she waited for Chase to take the lead, and fortunately he kept things simple.

They started by discussing the decor of the restaurant, as well as the movies advertised on the posters outside. They also talked about Rusty and how Chase hoped to find a kitten for Tommy and Missy Haines.

The Web site and the online newspapers she'd read had been wrong about him, she realized. Well, not about his skill, his daring and his aggressiveness on the track. But about him being anything but a kind and generous man—if also a roguish gentleman—any woman would be happy to date.

They ate salad with a homemade vinaigrette dressing, as well as pasta and grilled chicken with a zesty tomato and artichoke sauce.

As the meal was ending, Chase lifted the wine bottle and refilled Molly's glass. She rarely drank, so one glass of merlot had given her a warm buzz already.

Or had the buzz been a result of the handsome man who sat across from her?

Chase had been drawing smiles from her all evening, as well as stirring up feelings she hadn't experienced in more than a year. No, that wasn't true. She'd never experienced such a powerful physical attraction, such an incredible sense of wonder in her life. And she shouldn't be doing so now. But it felt good to let down her guard, to share a romantic dinner with a handsome man and to pretend there was something brewing between them.

"I'd like to date you," he said.

The breakneck change in topic made her blink. Then she realized he was serious. "We can't…do that, I—"

"Why not? I'm not a patient anymore."

"Yes, I know. But…you're a race car driver. I'd never be able to handle the danger, the risk."

"You wouldn't have to." A rebellious smile tugged one side of his lips. "I'd be the one handling that."

It sounded so simple, so matter-of-fact, but he didn't get it. And she feared a lot of men wouldn't. "Chase, if I allowed myself to care for you, I wouldn't be able to support what you do. Or who you are."

He paused for a moment, as though trying to make sense of it all. And she could understand why he'd have a problem with it. Many women probably found his career exciting, thrilling, but Molly wasn't one of them.

She'd seen the effects of car accidents, both personally and as a nurse in the hospital. And she knew what it felt like to lose almost everyone and everything she'd ever loved. It was a risk she wasn't willing to take.

She looked at him, hoping he understood and that they wouldn't have to discuss it any further. But something simmered in his eyes, something hot and stirring.

He reached for her hand and held it in a warm, solid grip. His thumb caressed her wrist, sending her pulse racing and her emotions soaring in a hundred different directions. His gaze locked on hers. "Then what do we do about *this?*"

He didn't have to explain what he meant by *this*. The

tension buzzed and swirled around them, just as it had been doing all evening, and she found it nearly impossible to shake off.

Reluctantly, she pulled her hand away. "I have no idea what to do about it. Ignore it, I guess."

"Then you're a lot stronger than I am."

That was doubtful. Right now, she felt like a ninety-pound weakling who was absolutely powerless to resist anything, but she'd be darned if she'd let him know that.

The waiter stopped by and asked if they'd like dessert, and they both declined. Then Chase paid the bill and stood.

"Come on," he said, waiting for her to rise. When she did, he slipped his arm around her to guide her out of the restaurant. The move seemed so natural, so right, that she nearly leaned against him.

Nearly, but not quite.

Still, her pulse was zipping along at breakneck speed, and her senses were spinning on a path of their own.

It was the wine, she told herself. And the romantic ambience of an extraordinary evening that she wasn't likely to ever experience again.

But try as she might, she still couldn't shake the effects Chase and their time together were having on her. And she wasn't sure that she wanted to.

On the walk home, their shoulders brushed a time or two more, and she had the urge to reach for his hand, to dive right in and become a couple.

How crazy was that?

If he had a desk job, if he worked from home, things would be different. It would be easier to consider dating him. But he had a wild and dangerous career that could, if something went wrong, leave him disabled or worse. And after everything she'd lost, she wasn't sure she could afford to risk her heart on a man like Chase.

By the time they reached her house, she didn't know if she should be relieved or sad. In spite of herself, she lingered on the porch rather than immediately heading inside and sending him on his way.

The scent of his aftershave, something manly and rugged, stirred up an unusual sense of freedom and adventure, and she found herself wanting to share a goodbye kiss so she would have something to hold on to after he was gone from her life.

Deciding to deal with any consequences her actions might bring, she placed her hand on his chest, felt the expensive fabric of his shirt, the steady beat of his heart and the vibrant male essence that filled him.

Meeting his gaze, she felt the connection they'd shared from the first time they'd talked at the hospital grow into an undeniable bond, one she could almost touch.

She raised her hand and touched his cheek, felt his solid, square jaw, the bristle of beard shadow.

He placed his fingers over hers as they rested on his cheek, then he tilted her hand outward and brought it to his mouth. He placed a kiss on her palm, sending an erotic rush of goose bumps along her arms.

The moist warmth of his breath nearly knocked her to her knees, and she placed her free hand on his shoulder to steady herself. She wanted to feel his arms around her, to absorb his woodsy scent. So she reached to the back of his neck, the locks of hair brushing her knuckles, and drew his face to hers.

As their lips touched, he pulled her into his embrace, and she held on tight, leaning into him and relishing a man's touch for the first time in what seemed like forever.

And it felt better than good; it felt right.

There they stood, kissing under the light of a three-quarter moon for all the neighborhood to see, yet it seemed as though they were the only two people in the world.

Her lips parted and her tongue sought his, seeking and tasting. Her eyes were closed but overhead the stars had surely exploded in a kaleidoscope of colors.

Across the way, a door opened and closed. And while she didn't care who saw them, who knew what she was doing, the sound was interference enough to force a decision.

She might be sorry for this tomorrow, but she drew her mouth from his, her breathing laced with desire.

"I don't normally do things like this," she said, as she dug in her purse and pulled out her key.

"I'm glad you did tonight."

She heard the humor in his voice, knowing that he was referring only to the kiss.

But then she unlocked the door, took him by the hand and led him inside.

Chase had been so sure that Molly was going to send him on his way after their heated kiss, so when she led him into the house, he was pleasantly surprised.

He'd be damned if he knew what he would have done if she'd sent him away, fully aroused and as frustrated as an adolescent on hormone overload—especially when the nearest cold shower was miles away.

His head was still spinning, his blood still pounding.

She'd left a light on in the living room when they'd left, and now, as he studied her in the soft glow, he was glad that she had.

That pretty black dress hugged her curves, showcasing what the hospital scrubs had hidden and revealing a beautiful woman any man would be proud to have on his arm. A sexual flush on her neck and chest told him she'd been just as affected by that kiss as he'd been.

She raked her fingers through the white-gold strands of her hair, and he realized he was…

What?

Temporarily smitten, he supposed.

"Did they teach you the fine art of kissing at nursing school?" he asked, trying to make light of something that was anything but.

"It's been a while," was all she said.

"I don't know about that," he argued. "If I had to guess, I'd say you must have been practicing day and night."

Her smile nearly knocked him to the floor, and he couldn't help closing the distance between them. He wrapped his arms around her, hoping to take up where they'd left off.

As he lowered his mouth to hers, her lips parted, and his control faded. The kiss deepened into something hot and demanding, something wild and free.

He closed his eyes, caught in a heady arousal of pounding hormones and blended scents as he tasted every inch of her soft, moist mouth, as his hands slid along the curve of her back, the slope of her hips.

A surge of desire nearly knocked him senseless, and he gripped her bottom and pulled her flush against him.

She whimpered in response, and her fingers threaded through his hair, drawing his lips closer, his tongue deeper.

When they came up for air, he caught her cheeks in his hand, his gaze snaring hers. "I've never wanted to make love to anyone as much as I want to with you."

And he wasn't just blowing smoke. In spite of having been married and being a happy and active bachelor for the better part of the past five years, he had to admit that it was true.

"I know that we're not suited to each other," she said breathlessly.

Oh, yeah? That kiss they'd just shared insisted otherwise.

"But we're both adults with needs," she added.

Something told him—warned him—that making love with Molly would be more than just sex, but he wasn't in any position to argue right now. Not when it appeared that she was going to give him a green light to the bedroom.

The emotional stuff could wait, although one thing was certain. He'd told her he wanted to date her, and after that kiss, he was sure he wouldn't have any reservations about making a commitment to her—at least for the time being.

Molly reached for his hand, then led him to her bedroom, a cozy space with pale green walls and a white goose-down comforter. When she reached the bed, she pushed back the spread and top sheet, then opened the drawer of her nightstand and pulled out a couple of condoms and set them where they'd be ready, waiting.

Then she turned her back to him and lifted her hair.

His fingers nearly fumbled as he unzipped her dress. Then he pushed the fabric off her shoulders and placed a kiss on her neck.

Her breath caught as she took a moment to savor the contact. She slid the garment off her body, allowing it to drop to the floor.

She turned and stood before him in a pair of lacy black panties and a matching bra.

He swallowed hard, his heart pounding furiously. He eased toward her, slowly. "You're beautiful, Nurse Molly."

She skimmed her fingers across his chest as she began to unbutton his shirt, sending a shiver through his nerve endings and a rush of heat through his blood.

No doubt about it, the lady knew what she wanted.

And so did he.

She tugged his shirttail out of his pants, and he took the lead, removing his shirt. When it was off, she reached behind her and unhooked her bra, releasing her breasts, the dusky tips peaked. He dropped to one knee to caress and kiss them, taking time to suckle one and nip it gently with his teeth.

She whimpered, swayed slightly and reached for his arm to steady herself.

Pleased with the effect he'd had on her, he stood, scooped her into his arms and laid her on the bed.

After ridding himself of his pants, he joined her, continuing to stroke, to kiss and to caress her until they were both overcome with desire.

He slipped off her panties and loved her with his hands and his mouth until they were both desperate for release.

"I need you inside me now," she said, her voice husky with desire.

He needed her, too.

In what seemed to be only a heartbeat, they were both naked. He reached for a foil packet and tore it open. If he'd been with anyone else, he might have checked the wrapping, the expiration date. But he was with a medical professional who was surely on top of those things.

Besides, he was also too far gone to give a damn about anything other than making love to Nurse Molly all night long.

When he'd taken care of the protection, he entered her, slowly at first, and as she arched to meet him, he thrust deeply, again and again. Her body responded to his, giving and taking until they were both breathless with need.

She cried out with her climax, her nails gripping his shoulders, scraping the skin. That's all it took to send him over the edge with her.

He shuddered as he released, riding the waves of pleasure.

If he'd ever had any question about whether Molly was the right woman to take home to meet his sponsors, the woman who'd not only appeal to their conservative natures, but who would be easy for him to commit to, he no longer had any doubts.

She'd said they weren't suited, but they'd just proven that statement wrong with the best sex he'd ever had.

Chase had no idea what he was feeling for Molly exactly, but he suspected it was more than physical.

Surely she felt it, too.

Of course, he had no way of knowing how long a relationship between them would last, but Molly had been the one to mention that they both had needs. So he suspected she'd agree to let things fall where they may.

And if she still claimed they weren't good for each other?

Well, then he'd just have to convince her otherwise.

As the dawn crept through a crack in the curtains, Molly lay curled in Chase's arms, her bottom nestled in his lap.

Last night had been incredible, and while she wasn't anywhere near as sexually experienced as he undoubtedly was, she didn't have to ask if it had been good for him. She'd seen it in his eyes, heard it in his voice, felt it in his embrace.

As a lover, Chase was too good to be true. And that's what had her confused this morning. She struggled with wanting more and knowing it would never work. A relationship with Chase Mayfield would make her face her biggest fear every day: losing another loved one to the cruel hand of fate.

The only way she could consider having more than a one-night stand with him would be to insist that he quit racing for good, but he would never do that.

How could he? Racing was an integral part of who he was, just as nursing defined her, which meant they didn't have a chance in the world of creating a lasting relationship, and they'd be crazy to even try.

So she tightened her armor a notch, determined to get her lust under control.

As she carefully pried herself out of his arms, intending to head for the bathroom to take a shower, he drew her back to him.

"Where are you going?" he asked, his voice graveled from sleep.

He obviously wasn't ready to end their night together, which ought to be comforting, but it wasn't. Not when reality dawned with the morning sun.

"I'm going to shower," she said. "Unless you want to take one first."

"No, that's okay." He reached out, touched her back, his fingers trailing against her skin as she continued to climb from bed.

She padded across the floor and into the bathroom, eager to close the door so she wouldn't have to see him, wouldn't have to wrestle the temptation to get back into bed and wrap her arms around him one more time.

Last night, she'd convinced herself that she could make love for the sake of sex alone. She'd needed the physical release.

But a warm knot had begun to grow in her chest each time Chase went out of his way to make things good for her, to find just the right spot to touch, to stroke.

Still, there was no way she could let things go on any longer. It would be tough enough to back out now and not suffer a broken heart.

The knot in her chest fisted tight, swelling and banging against her rib cage like a kicking-and-screaming child determined to have its own way.

"Damn," she muttered as she turned on the spigot and waited for the water to heat, fearing it was too late. That her heart would break anyway.

She'd known they were destined for this the first time she'd considered him to be more than a patient. She just hadn't realized how hard it would be to let him go. Chase had touched something deep inside her, something that had never been touched before.

Emotion clogged her throat and clouded her eyes, but she did her best to blink it back as she climbed under the pounding spray.

She wasn't sure how long she stayed in the shower, but no amount of water had been able to wash away the pain.

Sure, if Chase had another occupation, something safe that allowed him to live nearby, she could consider the possibilities. But he didn't have another job, and she was going to have to live with that.

She'd survive, though. She was a big girl; she knew the rules, the choices.

The repercussions.

So the decision was made. Making love had been a one-time thing. And she would make it clear that they were both better off that way.

After shutting off the water, she dried herself, brushed her teeth and returned to the bedroom wearing a towel turban on her wet head and a white fluffy robe wrapped around her body.

Her bare feet slowed as she entered and spotted Chase lying amidst the rumpled sheets.

Their gazes locked, and she did her best to smile. But a feeling of remorse settled over her as she watched him sit up in bed, his torso bare, his hair tousled in a sexy, after-the-loving way that reminded her of what they'd done, what she'd like to do again.

"Last night was special," he said, smiling.

It certainly had been.

Something sparked in his eyes, an emotion too fleeting to get a handle on.

She hoped that meant their lovemaking had touched something deep in his heart, too, but she couldn't afford to dream, to wish on stars that were doomed to burn out.

"I want you to know that I feel something for you," she admitted, "something that could easily break. And I want to end things before we get carried away."

His expression sobered. "I'm not sure I'm following you."

Molly sighed. "I'm not a risk-taker, Chase. My world is orderly and predictable, and I like it that way. The only way I'd be able to handle a relationship with you is if you gave up racing."

A muscle on the side of his eye twitched. "I don't like ultimatums."

"It isn't one. I'd never do that to you. But I lost my family in a car accident, and each day you climb behind the wheel, you put yourself in danger."

"I'm good at what I do."

"No doubt you are, but it's still a risk you take freely. And I probably worry more than most."

*Probably?* a small voice asked.

Okay, so her fears were a little over the top.

"We can work through this," he began.

She slowly shook her head. "No, we can't."

They seemed to be at an impasse until he said, "You can't tell me the sex wasn't good."

A slow smile pulled up her lips. "I doubt if I'll ever have better."

He climbed out of bed and reached for the pants he'd discarded on the floor. "You could expect it to be better if I was your lover."

"I'm sure you're right." She stooped and picked up his shirt, then handed it to him. "Did you want to shower before you go?"

"No, I'll do that at home."

She followed him to the front door, and that knot in her chest beat harder, putting up a struggle as it tried to stop her. But she knew a relationship with Chase was bound to end as soon as the racing season began.

And if she kissed him again, if they made love one last time, she risked falling head over heels for him, and then she'd be in a real fix. She'd die a little each time she heard his name, each time she learned of an upcoming race.

When they reached the door, she half expected him to give her a goodbye kiss, but he didn't. And maybe it was just as well. Look where it had gotten them last night.

"Drive safely," she said.

She hadn't just meant back to Houston. She'd meant every time he was on the track, every time he risked his life on the road.

At that, he stopped on the porch and turned to face her. His gaze slammed into hers. Then, as if he knew all that she felt, all that she feared, he brushed a kiss on her lips.

"If you're ever in Houston, give me a call," he said.

"I will."

He hesitated momentarily, as if he were struggling

with something, too. Then he kissed her one last time, a heart-thumping, hope-stirring kiss that would linger in her memory for a very long time.

## Chapter Seven

Molly's rejection sat in Chase's gut like a lump of engine sludge.

He'd known that she hadn't been eager to get involved with him in the first place, but he hadn't expected her to end it all after a marathon night of lovemaking—and before they'd been able to brew a morning pot of coffee.

As soon as they were both awake, she'd clearly rolled up the welcome mat, and he'd never been one to hang around when he wasn't wanted or appreciated—a remnant from his childhood, no doubt.

And as he'd lain in bed that morning, hearing her words, sensing the rejection, the shadow of a memory had ghosted over him, leaving him feeling unsettled and ready to bolt.

*What do* you *know,* his brother Phillip had once said to him. *You're nothing but a family accident.*

*Yeah,* Bobby had added, *Mom and Dad planned to stop with three kids, but then they went and messed up, and you came along. They even had to cancel our family vacation that year and every year after.*

Chase had flipped them off or some appropriate childish who-gives-a-crap response, but the truth had hurt. And as if knowing they'd found his Achilles' heel, his older brothers had prodded that soft spot time and again.

And the same uneasiness, that same sense of nothingness, had settled over him when Molly had told him that he wasn't the kind of guy she wanted to have in her life. Not that she'd come right out and said it in so many words, but Chase had read between the lines.

If the sex had been lousy, he might have understood it. But they'd gone through all the condoms she had and there was *no* way she'd been disappointed by their lovemaking.

Still, he'd gotten her message loud and clear. So he'd rolled out of bed and slipped into his pants, wishing all the while that he could come up with a better way to say goodbye. But he hadn't been able to think of one damn thing that wouldn't make it sound as though he was begging her to give him another chance. And Chase Mayfield didn't beg.

Not with his older brothers, not with his parents. Not with *anyone.*

Besides, Molly had said that the only way she'd get involved with him was if he gave up racing, and that was something else he'd never do. Racing was in his blood.

As Molly had stood in the bedroom that morning wearing a white robe, her skin moist and glowing from the shower, her hair wrapped in a towel, she'd been breathtakingly beautiful. But her words and her subdued tone hadn't been.

When he'd gotten ready to leave, she'd handed him his shirt and had watched while he put it on.

Had she been eager to see him go?

Or had she just tried to be helpful?

He'd probably never know for sure.

For the next couple of days, he tried to keep busy in Houston while making sure his sponsors hadn't gotten wind of any wild and reckless behavior—or his failed attempt at romance. But he hadn't been able to shake thoughts of Molly.

"You're better off without her," he told himself time and again, but he hadn't been able to buy it. He hadn't been ready for her to hand him his walking papers.

Yet something told him she hadn't been ready to hand them out, either. That there was something else going on, although he wasn't quite sure what it was.

Maybe he'd sensed that she felt something for him, like his parents had eventually come to care about the baby they hadn't really wanted. That was the reason he'd never run away from home, the reason he'd stuck it out. Instead, he'd rebelled when it hadn't been expected, made them proud when they'd thought for sure he wouldn't.

He'd kept them all wondering what would come next.

So that's the tack he'd taken with Molly.

After nearly a week, he'd returned to Brighton Valley to talk to her again. But he hadn't wanted to just show up on her stoop with his tail between his legs and a wishful look on his face. That had never been his style.

Instead, he'd carried a black-and-white kitten he'd found at an animal shelter. Then, when she answered the door, he'd acted as though they really had ended up friends, and that he was free to pop in whenever he wanted to.

"What do you think of this little guy?" he'd asked her.

"It's darling," she'd said, her face and her voice going all sweet and smoochy. And when she'd softened like that, his heart had done the same thing.

"What are you going to do with a kitten?" she'd asked.

"I'm going to take it to Tommy and Missy Haines."

"Shouldn't you run it by their mother first?"

"I was going to, but those poor kids don't have a lot, and they lost their other cat. How could their mother say no?"

She'd crossed her arms and lifted a single brow. "You might be right, but that's their mother's call to make."

And apparently, deciding whether Chase and Molly would become lovers again was Molly's decision to make.

"Do you want to ride with me to take this little guy to them? I'll leave him in the car until I get a chance to run it by their mom, if it makes you happy."

"I'm afraid I've got things to do this afternoon."

"That's too bad," he'd said. "I thought you would get a big kick out of seeing their faces when I give it to them."

She'd reached out and stroked the kitten's head. "I would have."

Well, he'd crashed and burned once more. And just like before, he'd been reluctant to leave until she gave him some reason to think they could make plans to see each other again.

But that hadn't happened, either.

"Are you doing okay?" he'd asked, hoping to peer through the veil that hid the emotion in her eyes.

"Yes, I'm fine."

She hadn't looked fine. She'd looked…sad. And he'd wondered if it had anything to do with him.

"Any regrets?" he'd asked, hoping she'd admit that her biggest one was letting him go.

"No. I'm glad we did what we did."

"Good." He was glad, too. And his only regret was that what they'd shared seemed destined to be a one-night fling.

But opening his guts any more than he'd already done wasn't going to do either one of them any good.

And while he knew it was over, that they were finished, something continued to draw him to her. Something that suggested she'd ended things, but that her heart hadn't been in it.

Still, he'd left that day with his tail tucked between his legs just a bit tighter than he'd been comfortable with. And he'd managed to keep himself occupied for another week or so, but that was it.

The harder he'd tried to stay away from Molly, the more he wanted to see her.

So now it was time for a showdown.

As part of a well-thought-out game plan, he checked into the Brighton Valley Motor Inn and decided to stick around town until she saw things his way.

Three weeks after her one and only date with Chase, Molly sat in the kitchen, writing out checks to pay her bills: rent, utilities and a medical expense her health insurance hadn't picked up because her deductible hadn't been met.

It seemed that the tenth came around faster each month, but certain things were a part of the life, like billing cycles and...

Menstrual cycles.

Her hand froze in the middle of her signature as she realized it had been a while since she'd had one.

How long?

She used the calendar on the back of the check register, counting back to the first of last month and thinking that she was rarely late.

For a moment, she wondered if she could be pregnant, but quickly shook off the possibility. She and Chase had used condoms—several of them.

There had to be another explanation.

For one thing, her job could be stressful, which might have an adverse effect on her regularity. Of course, it never had before.

But there was also the matter of the hospital's financial concerns, which were more than a little troubling. Ever since she'd become friends with Dr. Nielson, the money issues facing the hospital and causing Betsy stress had also applied pressure to Molly, who couldn't help herself from worrying on her friend's behalf.

And on top of that, no matter how much she tried to convince herself that she had everything—including her heart—under control, Chase had also created tension in her life.

She was missing him in spite of knowing that it was best if they didn't see each other anymore. Add that to the fact that he'd been showing up on her doorstep on her days off—for one reason or another—and it only made things worse.

Again pregnancy crossed her mind, but as she'd done the first time it had, she reminded herself that they'd been responsible, that they'd used protection. So she really ought to give her period a few more days to show up.

But no method of birth control was one hundred percent effective, and Molly's curiosity mounted. She liked her life to be predictable, and she went to extraordinary lengths to make sure it stayed that way. Some might call her a control freak, but she didn't care. If she'd gotten pregnant that night, she wanted time to think, to prepare.

A baby would certainly complicate her life. Not that she didn't like children. She was actually good with them in a hospital setting, but she hadn't considered having any of her own. She was so wrapped up in her career that she didn't have time for a family.

Of course, she was probably jumping to faulty conclusions, but either way, she was going to have to put her mind to rest.

So she returned her checkbook to her purse, stacked the outgoing mail on the kitchen counter, then rode her bike to the market. Once there, she picked up a box of cereal, a carton of milk, a roll of paper towels and a home pregnancy test.

She hadn't needed the cereal or the other items, but she hoped they would mask her real purpose for the shopping trip.

It seemed as though all eyes were on her and her purchases while she stood in the checkout line, but when she glanced up, she didn't see anyone but the cashier, a fiftysomething ash-blonde who seemed to be too bothered by a hangnail to give it any thought.

In less than thirty minutes, Molly was home again. After leaving her bike on the front porch and securing the lock, she entered the house and put away her groceries. Then she carried the testing apparatus and the instruction sheet into the bathroom.

Surely she wasn't pregnant, she argued one more time. But had they gotten careless as the night wore on? Had one of the condoms broken?

The box had been in her drawer for ages, ever since she'd dated Randy. Or had it been there even longer than that?

For the life of her, she couldn't remember. And right now, the only thing on her mind was the memory of their lovemaking, which was never far from her conscious thought. Unable to help herself, she relived each stroke, each caress, each heated kiss until she missed Chase so badly she wanted to tell him she'd been wrong.

But she knew better than that.

Of course if she was pregnant with his baby, she'd be drawn into his life anyway, and she'd be hard-pressed to forget her fears.

"Oh, for Pete's sake," she uttered as she got on with the process, then awaited the results.

With each second that silently tick-tocked through the room, time stretched and strained like a frayed rubber band, tighter and tighter until it was ready to snap.

Finally, a little pink dot formed, mocking every attempt Molly had made to convince herself she hadn't conceived. She blinked her eyes a couple of times, hoping to clear her vision, hoping to see that the result screen had remained blank.

But that bright pink spot wasn't going anywhere.

Molly stared at the testing apparatus for the longest time, hoping for a different outcome until she was forced to accept the truth.

She was pregnant—with Chase Mayfield's baby.

The next day, with the news of her pregnancy still rumbling in her heart and rolling through her mind, Molly dressed for work.

She was running late, which didn't happen very often. Had it been any other workday, she might have passed on breakfast, opting to pick up a bagel and coffee in the hospital cafeteria later, but she forced herself to drink a glass of milk and eat a banana while she walked the few short blocks to Brighton Valley Medical Center.

The sun was warm overhead, and birds chirped in the treetops. It was hard not to think of new life and renewal, even if she was still trying to wrap her mind around the fact that her little world and the future she'd mapped out for herself were about to change.

Sure, there were other options. She could give the baby up to a couple who would provide it a happy, two-parent home, but she'd never do that. This pregnancy might be unplanned and a bit inconvenient, but the more she thought about having a baby, a son or daughter to love, the more it brought a smile to her face. It was almost as if God was giving her a second chance to have the family that had been taken from her.

As was her habit, she entered the hospital grounds by cutting through the gardens, where she spotted Betsy seated on a bench.

The doctor was clearly taking a break, and while Molly thought about allowing the woman privacy, she approached anyway.

"Good morning," she said.

Betsy looked up and smiled, although her expression was shrouded by whatever had caused her to seek privacy.

"Is something wrong?" Molly asked.

"No, I just wanted some time to think. My attorney called and told me that Joe is being sentenced today, and that he'll probably be spending the next ten years or so at McCrea."

The state penitentiary, Molly realized.

Betsy had once been married to a man living two lives, a man who'd not only deceived his business partners, but his unsuspecting wife, too. He'd been arrested, tried and found guilty of embezzling millions from the company. But he'd taken a lot more than money from Betsy.

"Thank goodness we never had kids," Betsy said. "It would have made things so much worse."

Molly assumed she meant that it would be tough to explain to the children what their father had done. Or maybe she meant that a divorce would have been more painful with children and their feelings involved. It would have been harder to make a clean break.

Kids certainly changed things, just as Molly's baby was about to change her life—and in ways she couldn't yet imagine.

As she'd done several times since learning she was pregnant, she wondered what kind of a father Chase would be. She'd have to tell him about the baby, of course. But for now it was Molly's secret.

She glanced at Betsy, half tempted to confide in her friend, but she was afraid to share the news with anyone. Maybe it was best to keep it to herself—at least, until she told Chase.

"Well," Molly said, "I've dawdled enough. My shift starts in a few minutes, so I'd better get to work."

Three hours later, Molly sat at the third-floor nurses' desk, completing the discharge forms for Mrs. Wentworth, a woman recovering from an appendectomy in room 302.

The elevator doors opened, and Molly looked up. She spotted Chase getting out with a colorful bouquet of flowers in his hand.

Her first thought was that he'd come to see one of the patients, although she didn't think there was anyone still here that he could have met during his own stay.

He wasn't from Brighton Valley or the surrounding area, either, so the visit struck her as surprising.

"Fancy seeing you here," she said. "Who are you here to see?"

"Just you, Nurse Molly." He flashed her a crooked grin and handed her the bouquet.

"You shouldn't have done that," she said, yet she took the flowers from him anyway.

"Have you got time to join me for lunch?" he asked.

She wanted to tell him no, to insist that she'd meant what she'd said about them not getting involved. But as much as she wished otherwise, having a baby bound them together anyway, even if marriage or romance wasn't in their future.

Unless, of course, he wasn't interested in being a part of the child's life.

She glanced at the clock on the wall, realizing that she could take a break if she wanted to.

Maybe it wouldn't hurt to have a quick bite with him in the cafeteria, to lay a few ground rules for their *friendship.*

"Sure," she said. "Let me talk to Carol and make sure she's able to cover for me."

Ten minutes later, after placing the flowers in the break room and deciding to deliver them later to a patient who hadn't had any visitors during her stay, Molly went with Chase to the cafeteria, where they each filled a tray. He paid the bill at his insistence, and they took their food to a table in the back corner.

Chase had chosen a cheeseburger and fries, as well as a slice of berry pie for dessert, while Molly tried to be more health-conscious than usual by choosing grilled chicken, steamed vegetables, fruit and a glass of milk.

Her food was good, but his juicy burger looked a whole lot tastier.

"Most people prefer not to eat hospital food if they don't have to," she said.

"Yeah, well most people don't have friends who work here."

He'd thrown out the *friends* line as though he had no plans to change that, but she wouldn't budge. She couldn't. Of course, couples who chose to have platonic relationships probably hadn't slept together and experienced the best sex they'd ever had, so it might prove to be difficult.

Not that Molly was saying Chase hadn't experienced better. He really hadn't come right out and said either way, although she suspected he'd rated it pretty high.

"I was serious about not having a relationship with you," she said.

"I'm sure you were."

So what was he trying to do? Wear her down? Change her mind?

She lowered her voice. "Making love again isn't an option, either."

"Do you plan to stay celibate the rest of your life?" he asked.

She'd gone more than a year without it the last time, and she'd survived. But Randy hadn't been anywhere near as good a lover as Chase had been. And now that she'd had better—a whole *lot* better—she wasn't so sure she'd like to go another entire year...

Boy. Going without sex that long sounded almost unhealthy.

Still, dating Chase in any way, shape or form would make her crazy.

"I care about you," she admitted. "A *lot*. And the other night was off the charts. At least, it was for me."

His eyes glistened, a result of some good old male pride, she suspected.

She let him revel in it as she continued her carefully planned speech. "But I can't allow myself to get involved with you romantically. I'd be a nervous wreck each time you got on the track, each time you risked your life."

"I'm very good at what I do, Molly. It's not as risky as it might seem."

She lifted a brow in disbelief, but held back a response.

"Sometimes you have to take a chance in life."

"Are you suggesting I take one on us? I'd clearly worry myself crazy, and that's a fact. So why should I jump into something I know won't work? I see only misery for me. And for you, too. Because somewhere along the line, I'd probably issue that ultimatum you don't want to hear. And then, instead of you remembering me fondly and our night together as special, you'd be left with bad feelings, bad memories."

"There's got to be a way for us to work through this," he insisted.

"There isn't." If he continued to race—and she wouldn't expect him to stop—there wasn't any hope at all.

"But—"

"No, Chase." She reached out and placed her hand on his forearm, her fingers gripping him, desperate for him to hear her out. "I need you to understand this. I can end things now and come out emotionally okay. But if I let things go any further, I'd only end up with a broken heart. And I'm sorry. I'm just not up for getting hurt that way. Not again."

She'd suffered enough losses in her life. And if she didn't protect herself from more, who else would?

She watched his eyes carefully, hoping he'd heard her words, that he'd gotten the message.

Chase Mayfield was the one man who would make her deal with her biggest fears on an almost daily basis.

Fears she couldn't risk facing.

The only trouble was, it was too late. She was very close to falling in love with him already, and her heart had already suffered a noticeable crack.

## *Chapter Eight*

A few days later, Chase met with Gerald Barden at a coffee shop just outside of Wexler for what Gerald had insisted was "a chance to catch up."

They talked about everything but the topic of their last couple of meetings: the ultimatum Chase had been given. But Chase knew it was bound to come up eventually.

Finally, as their meal, a late lunch, was winding down, Gerald leaned back in his seat. "That was a nice thing you did."

"What's that?"

"Paying that kid's medical bill."

Chase shrugged it off. Initially, he'd wanted to impress his sponsor and to take advantage of some good press for a change. But the truth was, he'd actually enjoyed helping Diana Haines and her kids. And he'd gotten a kick out of Sudsy and Howard, the two old men who'd become the self-appointed watchmen of the Lone Oak trailer park.

"Other than that," Gerald added, "you've managed to stay out of the news, so it looks like you took our little chat to heart."

Yeah, well, being submissive hadn't been intentional, but that's the way it had panned out. Besides, Chase had bigger fish to fry these days, and impressing Molly beat the hell out of trying to impress his sponsors.

"We're having a barbecue at the ranch on Sunday," Gerald said. "It'd be nice if you'd make a showing."

"I'll stop by if I can." Chase wasn't going to make any promises, especially when he knew that Molly had Sundays off.

Then a lightbulb went on.

Ever since Molly had admitted that she was afraid something might happen to Chase on the track, he'd been giving her some space, hoping she'd change her mind. After all, she'd said that she cared for him, and he suspected her feelings might go a little deeper than that.

Sure, he understood that she was afraid of losing someone again. But living her life in fear wasn't healthy. And the sooner she came to realize that, the better.

If she would only give them a chance, he had a feeling it would all work out—somehow. Besides, he didn't like taking no for an answer. Not without a fight.

Maybe if he could introduce her to the racing world, if she better understood his life, they could work through things. And what better way than to bring her to the barbecue at Gerald's ranch.

"Would you mind if I brought a date?" he asked.

Gerald arched a bushy gray brow. "You know that Pammy will probably be there."

Chase knew what he was getting at. "Don't worry about Molly and Pamela. If those two met as strangers anywhere else, they'd take a real liking to each other."

Gerald took a chug of his iced tea. "Then if that's the case, bring this Molly along. I'd like to meet her."

"I'll have to see if she's available," Chase said. "She's a nurse, and her schedule varies."

On top of that, he'd also have to convince her to go with him, which wasn't going to be easy.

She seemed to think that she'd dealt with the death of her family, but that wasn't the case. Not if she was afraid she'd lose someone she'd come to care about. And since there was definitely something brewing between them, he figured she was going to worry about him on the track anyway.

Sure, something could go wrong. There were inherent risks in all professional sports. However, Chase was good at what he did. He was aware of his skills on the track, as well as those of the other drivers.

Whether Molly knew it or not, he was a lot safer than she realized. So in spite of her reluctance, he was determined to win her over, to see if what he was feeling for her was real. And if it helped her get over her fears, which he really hoped would happen, then it was a win-win for them both.

He'd just have to turn on the charm.

If Molly would let her guard down and agree to go

to Gerald's barbecue, if she'd go out with him, maybe even sleep with him again…

Okay, so there were no maybes about it. He definitely wanted to take her to bed.

When the meal and their meeting was over, Gerald climbed into his black pickup, and Chase slid behind the wheel of the rental sedan he'd been driving. Normally he'd prefer to drive something nicer, something flashier, but for now, he'd decided it was in his best interest to remain not only under the radar, but also out of the limelight.

Racing season would be starting soon, and he needed to connect with Molly while things were relatively quiet and normal.

He'd tried his best to give her as much space as he could, but he didn't want to risk finding out that the old adage "out of sight, out of mind" was true.

So he'd taken her flowers the other day, telling her it was a token of their friendship. Even at the hospital, with her hair pulled back in a clip and wearing a pair of pink scrubs, she'd been as pretty as she'd been the night they'd eaten at Cara Mia's. And if anything, Chase was growing more and more convinced that what he was feeling for her was real and lasting, even if she was still dragging her feet.

Hey, she'd kept the flowers he'd given her. If she'd really wanted to end things, she could have refused to take them.

On his way back to the motor lodge, where he'd been holed up while he was trying to convince Molly they should be dating, he decided to stop by her house again. It was Thursday, which was usually her day off.

And who set up that schedule? he wondered. Thursdays and Sundays off? She didn't even get two days in a row. What kind of break was that?

When he turned left and drove down Johnston Lane, he parked in front of her place, a yellow stucco house with white trim and a gingerbread-style flower box adorning the living room window. He left his car curbside and followed the sidewalk to the front porch, where her bicycle rested, secured by a lock.

He suspected she was home, but when he knocked at the door, he didn't get an answer.

Was she out back?

Curious, he couldn't help stepping off the porch, walking to the window, cupping his hands around his eyes and peering through the glass into the living room.

The lamp was on, which didn't make sense considering it was still daytime. But now that he thought about it, she did that when she was expecting to come home after dark.

"Can I help you?" a female voice asked.

Chase turned away from Molly's window, only to find a silver-haired woman glaring at him as though she'd caught a peeping Tom.

"I'm a friend of Molly's," he said.

The woman, stooped from age, straightened the best she could. "What's your name?"

"Chase Mayfield."

"The race car driver?" She cocked her grayed head slightly and squinted her eyes, checking him out.

"Yes, ma'am. That's me."

The lines on her face softened as she broke into a grin. "Well, I'll be darned. I'm a big stock car fan."

Chase reached out a hand and greeted her officially. "It's always nice to meet someone who appreciates racing."

"I'm Wanda Carlisle, Molly's neighbor." She looked him up and down, and her eyes glimmered with humor. "Are you that fellow I saw her kissing on this very porch a few weeks back?"

Chase chuckled. "I sure hope it was me. I'd hate to think she's seeing some other guy."

Wanda laughed. "If you're worried about that, it's plain to see that you don't know Molly very well."

Maybe not, but he was working on that.

Wanda crossed her arms, that grin never leaving her craggy face. "I'm happy to know she's got a beau. For a gal as pretty as she is, she sticks too close to home. She really needs to get out of the house and kick up her heels every now and then."

"I couldn't agree more," Chase said, thinking he'd do what he could to remedy that and appreciating the fact that Wanda would be cheering him on when he did.

The elderly woman took a few steps to the side so that she could place her hand on the railing that led to the porch, as though needing the support. "Molly's a wonderful person and the perfect neighbor, but she's a workaholic, and I don't think that's healthy."

Was that her real problem? Chase wondered. Was she too committed to her job and unable to cultivate a life for herself when her free time was limited to Thursdays and Sundays?

Wanda lifted an arthritic finger and pointed it at Chase. "Now don't get me wrong. I admire the nursing profession, but up until you came along, she had very little life outside that hospital. And what's worse, someone keeps calling her to come in and work on her days off, just like they did this morning."

"She's at work today?" he asked.

The woman grumbled something indiscernible and slowly shook her head. "You'd think Brighton Valley Medical Center would have other nurses they could call. But I suspect they don't bother since it's usually a given that Molly will say yes."

Oh yeah? Well, she certainly found it easy to say no to him.

But that was okay. He would just have to wear her down with smiles and flowers and invitations to dinner.

"It was nice meeting you," he told Wanda.

"Same here."

"Well," he said, making his leave, "if you'll excuse me, I need to get going."

She watched as he began to head for his sedan. "Where are you off to?"

He was glad that Wanda was concerned about Molly, but she was still the classic nosy neighbor. He flashed his unwitting cohort a smile. "Looks like I'll have to go to the hospital if I want to spend a little time with my girl."

While covering for Sara Mendez in the E.R., Molly again had the opportunity to work with Betsy. And as usual, the time had passed quickly in a busy emergency setting.

They'd had a stroke victim earlier who'd been admitted and sent up to the fourth floor, as well as a guy who'd nearly severed his finger with a Skil saw at work. There'd been a lot of blood, and as Betsy had unwrapped the shop rag from the patient's hand, Molly had suffered a wave of nausea. For a moment, she'd even felt faint.

Sure, she'd had that problem a time or two in nursing school, but she'd gone years without an adverse physical reaction and hadn't expected one today.

She suspected that pregnancy hormones were at play, and she made up her mind to decline any more time in the E.R. than necessary, since that's where she was more apt to see the types of injuries or conditions that could make her woozy or sick.

They'd managed to stop the man's bleeding, but Betsy had called in a surgeon who specialized in hands to actually suture the wound. She'd thought that he'd damaged the tendons, and she'd been right.

Next, they'd dealt with a drug overdose victim, as well as a fifty-two-year-old golfer who'd driven his cart into a tree, fallen out and broken his shoulder. Molly had smelled alcohol on his breath and wondered if there was a law against driving on a golf course while intoxicated, but shrugged it off when she took a second whiff and suffered another flash of nausea.

All in all, it had been a busy afternoon. But right now, while there was a lull in the E.R., Betsy chose to take a dinner break. Molly, who was able to clock out and head home, decided to join her.

Betsy poked her fork into her salad. "I really appreciate you being able to come in at a moment's notice."

"I know you wouldn't have called if you hadn't needed me." Molly took a bite of her turkey sandwich, thinking it didn't taste nearly as good as it had looked just minutes ago.

"It's always nice working with you," Betsy added, "which is a real perk for me. It's a treat to have both lunch and dinner together."

"Thanks. I'm glad you feel that way. But to be honest, I'm probably going to say no the next time I'm asked to work in the E.R."

"Why?" Betsy asked. "Is it bothering you worse than before?"

"Yes, but not for the same reason."

Betsy merely studied her across the table, waiting for a better explanation.

"I'm pregnant," Molly admitted. "And I nearly lost my cookies when the guy with the lacerated hand came in."

Betsy's fork froze in mid-motion. "I didn't realize you were seeing anyone special."

"I'm not."

Betsy's brow formed a V, and Molly realized that it probably had sounded as though she'd had a one-night stand with a complete stranger or that she'd gone to a sperm bank.

She took a fortifying breath, then slowly let it out. "I probably ought to clarify that. I know who the father is, but I'm not going to marry him. It was just one of those things, and I should have been more careful."

The V in Betsy's brow still hadn't completely gone away. "More careful with birth control? Or more careful in your choice of men?"

"Both, I guess. And now, what I thought was going to be a one-night thing, has turned out to be more long-lasting than I'd expected."

"I guess it's safe to say that the sex was disappointing."

"Unfortunately, that wasn't the case."

Betsy speared a cherry tomato with her fork and popped it into her mouth. "So if the sex was satisfying, what's wrong with the guy?"

"We're just…not very well-suited." Molly placed her uneaten sandwich back on her plate, but as she scanned her tray, none of her other food choices looked too appealing.

"Are you going to tell me who he is?" Betsy asked.

"I'm not sure if I should. I haven't told him about the baby yet. In fact, you're the only one who knows. I'm not very far along, so I'd kind of like to keep it under wraps for another month or two."

As if on cue, Chase strode into the cafeteria. For a moment, Molly wondered if she'd conjured his image. Just in case, she blinked her eyes, but no such luck.

He scanned the room, then, spotting Molly, strode toward her with a heart-strumming grin.

Betsy, who'd noticed Molly's far-off gaze, looked over her shoulder. When she recognized Chase, she turned her attention back to Molly and smiled. "Let me guess. Your one-night fling was with one of our patients."

"A *former* patient," Molly corrected.

"Well, if you were in the market for a daddy, I'd say you made a great choice. Genetically speaking, your baby is going to be one cute kid."

Molly lowered her voice so she wouldn't risk being

overheard. "Conception was the last thing on my mind that night."

Betsy laughed. "I'm sure it was. Chase Mayfield is a gorgeous man and a real charmer."

Molly reached for her napkin and blotted her mouth as though the movement could still the conversation as well as the thoughts and memories it had provoked.

As the handsome stock car driver reached their table, his smile broadened, setting off a pair of dimples that could charm the panties off a woman if she'd let them. "Good afternoon, ladies."

Molly's heart took a flying leap, then made a swan dive into the pit of her tummy.

Trying her best to ignore her physical reaction to Chase's presence, she glanced down at her tray, wondering why she'd chosen such unappealing food. She pushed it aside, then turned to Chase and tossed him a wry grin. "You're not stalking me, are you?"

"Since when do friends stalk each other?"

Molly, who'd made the comment tongue in cheek, let it go. Chase didn't give off any weird or scary vibes, although he certainly seemed to show up when she least expected him.

Didn't he live in Houston? Why did it seem that he was hanging out in Brighton Valley these days?

"What time are you off?" he asked her.

"I'm off now. Why?"

"That's perfect."

Molly leaned forward and placed her forearms on the table where her tray had once sat. "Perfect for what?"

"That movie we'd wanted to see is previewing tonight."

"What movie?"

"The one we talked about at Cara Mia's. We saw the poster on the walk home. Remember?"

They'd seen several posters that night. "I'm sorry. I'm drawing a blank."

"The romantic comedy," he said.

"Oh, yeah."

"When was the last time you went to a movie?" he asked.

Molly glanced at Betsy, who seemed to be enjoying this conversation a whole lot more than she ought to.

"It sounds like a good movie to me." Betsy pushed her chair back and stood. "Have fun."

"Where are you going?" Molly asked, wishing Betsy would stick around. She liked having a third party to defuse any talk of romance.

"I need to stop by the lab on my way back to the E.R. So I'll see you later."

When Betsy left them alone, Chase said, "So what do you say? Will you go with me?"

Molly really ought to hold firm, to tell him that he was barking up the wrong tree. But she hadn't seen a movie in ages, and it was beginning to sound like a good idea. "Okay, I'll go."

But there wouldn't be a sleepover afterward. She couldn't risk letting their relationship go in that direction again. And quite frankly, the movie was risky enough.

"I've got my car in the visitor's lot," he said. "Did you drive or walk today? I noticed your bike back at the house."

"A guy with a mobile detailing unit came to the hospital today, and I had him wash my car." It had saved her from driving across town, which is what she usually had to do when the car got dirty.

"I'll meet you at my house," she said. "I need to change clothes."

"All right." He offered her a dashing, look-who's-in-the-winner's-circle smile. "I'll see you in a few minutes."

Then he swept out of the cafeteria as quickly as he'd swept in.

It wasn't a date, she'd wanted to argue. But there was no one left to listen.

And like it or not, it certainly felt like one.


As Chase and Molly walked out of the theater, he was in no hurry to end their night together.

"That was a great movie," he said.

"I really enjoyed it, too. Thanks for encouraging me to go."

Maybe one day she'd thank him for being a little pushy and persistent about dating her, too.

As they walked through the outdoor mall, he spotted an ice cream shop up ahead.

She had to be hungry. He'd noticed how she'd only picked at her food in the cafeteria. And when he bought them popcorn at the movie and a couple of sodas, she'd only reached into the bucket once or twice and she'd only sipped at the cola.

He'd also noticed that she was big on exercise, since she liked to walk and ride her bike. He supposed being a nurse made her health-conscious.

As they neared the pink-and-white-trimmed shop, he nudged her arm. "How about an ice cream cone?"

He'd expected her to balk at the sugar or fat content, but she surprised him.

"You know, that sounds great. I love ice cream."

He placed a hand on her back, allowing her to enter in front of him.

As he followed her into the sweetly scented shop, he was reminded of childhood, bubble gum and lollipops. Bringing a date to a place like this was a first for him, and he was glad he was having the experience with Molly.

A teenage boy stood behind the glass refrigerator case that provided a multitude of choices. "Can I help you?"

"What would you like?" Chase asked Molly.

"A single scoop of vanilla."

"Are you kidding?" he asked. "That's too bland. Look at some of this stuff." He pointed to a carton of olive-green ice cream with brightly colored speckles in it. "That one's called Martian Delight. Now there's a cone with attitude."

She laughed and addressed the kid behind the counter. "Plain vanilla sounds much better to me. With a sugar cone, please."

"You got it," the boy said.

She turned to Chase. "How about you? Maybe a scoop of Martian Delight topped off with some Cherry Bomb Freeze?"

"I don't need *that* much attitude," he said, grinning. "But since I'm a chocolate fiend, I'm going to get a triple-decker rocky road."

When they'd both been served and Chase paid the tab, they carried their frozen concoctions outside and began the walk back to Molly's house.

The evening sky was clear, providing a panoramic display of constellations for stargazers wanting to connect the celestial dots. But Chase didn't comment on them. No need to get mushy and romantic, he decided. Yet he couldn't shake the feeling that tonight was almost magical with Molly at his side.

"What are the chances that you'd be able to take off on Saturday?" he asked her.

"Pretty good, since Sara just traded me days, leaving me my first weekend off in a long time. Why do you ask?"

"Because my mom is having a little family party on Saturday afternoon. It's my dad's birthday, and I thought you might like to join us."

A flash of irritation crossed her face. "I told you," she said, "that I don't want to date you."

"I know what you said. I also know that you care about me and the feelings are mutual. So I thought you might like to meet my family. That way, maybe you'll see that I'm not as wild and reckless as the papers have made me out to be."

"I believe you," she said, taking a lick of her cone. "Otherwise, you would have chosen a more adventurous flavor of ice cream. Chocolate is almost as tame as vanilla."

"Not when you add nuts and marshmallows," he argued, his grin turning into a full-on smile.

They continued to munch on their cones, their steps slow but steady. She didn't appear to be racing home, so he figured she was enjoying their time together, just as he was. And, interestingly enough, she hadn't completely nixed the birthday invitation yet.

He liked the idea of taking her home. Ever since his last brother had gotten married, he'd felt like the odd man out at family events. In fact, even when he'd been married to Pamela, she hadn't enjoyed socializing with his sisters-in-law, saying they didn't have much in common.

Molly, he realized, was more down to earth than Pamela and would fit in with the Mayfield clan a whole lot better.

"Where do your parents live?" she asked.

"In Garnerville. It's not too far from here. Maybe an hour or so."

She seemed to give his invitation some thought, which was a good sign, he decided.

"We'll see," she eventually said.

That was good enough for him.

They'd both finished their ice cream by the time they arrived at her house.

Chase wasn't sure what to expect—an invitation to come inside, he hoped. But she remained on the porch, her back to the door.

"Thanks for tonight," she said. "I had a nice time."

"Apparently, not nice enough to invite me in for a nightcap."

She looked down. "I don't think that's a good idea, Chase."

Yeah, well he disagreed, although he figured he'd made some leeway today, so he decided not to push.

But that didn't mean he wouldn't try to steal a kiss.

If there was one thing to be said about Chase, it was that when he set his mind on a goal, he didn't take *no* for an answer. And he'd set his mind on Molly.

So he cupped her face with his hands, drawing her

gaze to his. The soft yellow bulb in the porch light bathed them in a romantic glow.

"Let's take things slow and easy, Nurse Molly. We jumped into the heavy stuff a little too early, but I'm willing to backpedal. And I'd like to come up with some sort of compromise—to make you feel better about a relationship with me."

Her eyes glistened, and her lips parted.

That was all the come-on he needed, and he lowered his mouth to hers.

## Chapter Nine

Molly knew she shouldn't let Chase kiss her, but she couldn't help it. As his lips brushed hers, she kissed him back, closing her eyes and losing herself in the moment.

He tasted of ice cream, a heady blend of chocolate and vanilla. She'd expected him to come on strong, resulting in a heated rush and a heart-spinning demand for more.

Yet instead he kissed her sweetly, gently. And while the public display wasn't filled with the same hot passion that had driven her to take him inside and lead him to her bedroom, it still weakened her knees and stirred her blood.

As his hands slid up and down her back, he nipped at her lip, and she nearly fell apart in his arms. Chase Mayfield was one heck of a kisser, and while he didn't do a single thing that would have caused any of her neighbors to raise a brow in surprise, Molly's desire for more was enough to bring on a flush and make her wonder if they should remain outside for all the world to see.

When the kiss finally ended, when he drew his mouth from hers, she continued to lean into him, craving his warmth, yearning for something she couldn't define.

The kiss, as sweet as it was, had still left her unbalanced, out of breath and wanting more.

Okay, so kissing Chase had been a crazy thing to do if she planned to send him on his way—and she still did. But he'd been wearing her down over the past week, softening her defenses.

Leaving her vulnerable.

Truth be told, she'd been missing him, missing this. And after such a wonderful date—a movie, ice cream and a romantic walk home on a star-filled night—she hadn't been able to resist kissing him one more time, making a memory that would last through what was sure to be a long, lonely night.

Besides, Chase had told her he was willing to compromise, which had to mean he would at least consider giving up racing. Maybe he thought he could do something less dangerous, like working in the pit.

She could invite him inside, she supposed. She could suggest that they discuss the compromise he was willing to make, but she didn't trust herself not to sleep with him again. Because if she did, she might topple off the ledge of indecision on which she balanced and lose her heart to him completely.

For a woman who tried to remain in control of her life and her destiny, Chase was a real temptation to throw caution to the wind.

"Vanilla never tasted so good," he whispered, his warm, jagged breath taunting her. "No wonder you like it so much."

She didn't know about anything right now, other than liking *him* way more than she should. More than was good for her.

"Don't make a habit out of this," she said, slowly and reluctantly pulling out of his embrace.

"A habit out of what?"

"Good-night kisses."

"I'm afraid I can't commit to that." A boyish grin stretched across his face, and she suspected that had been his plan all along.

Watch out, she warned herself. If she wasn't careful, Chase Mayfield would be a hard habit to break.

Chase called Molly the next morning and again asked if she'd go to the birthday party. She didn't think it over very long before she finally agreed. After all, her child would be related to the Mayfields, and even if Chase decided not to be a part of the baby's life, she wanted to know more about his family.

By the time he pulled up in front of her house on Saturday, she'd tried on several outfits, none of which looked or felt right. If she and Chase did manage to reach some kind of compromise, if they did continue to see each other, she was going to have to go shopping.

She'd finally settled on a white blouse and a pair of black slacks that seemed to be a little tighter in the waist than they'd been the last time she'd worn them.

Instead of being annoyed—or blaming the half-eaten

carton of rocky road in her freezer, an impulse buy she'd made at the grocery store yesterday—she told herself it was because her baby was growing bigger, that the pregnancy was strong.

She'd combed her hair and carefully applied some lipstick and mascara. Then, for the first time ever, she'd looked into the jewelry box that had once belonged to her mother and chosen a pearl necklace and matching earrings, simple but elegant studs.

Having a part of her mom with her today brought on a smile, rather than the wave of sadness it might have stirred up years ago. She wasn't sure if the pleasure had anything to do with Chase, the baby or just the passage of time.

When she opened the door and spotted Chase on her porch, she saw a smile light his face. "You look really pretty."

"Thanks." She didn't dare tell him how long she'd stewed over what to wear and that she felt relieved to know that he was pleased with her choice.

He nodded toward the curb, where an unfamiliar car—something red and sporty—was parked. "I finally picked out something to replace that Corvette I totaled."

A clammy shiver ran up and down her back, and her tummy knotted.

She'd seriously pondered telling him that they ought to take two cars today, but she'd just about talked herself out of it.

That is, until now.

She'd always been uneasy riding in a car, although she pushed herself to do it whenever necessary. But she rarely rode as a passenger.

When she was behind the wheel, she controlled the speed, she looked ahead and avoided danger. But as a passenger, she was stuck, left in the hands of fate.

"Can I drive?" she asked.

"My new Corvette?" he asked. "Do you know how to use a stick?"

No. She was lost in anything other than an automatic.

"I meant that we could take my car." She clutched the shoulder strap of her purse, running her fingers along the braided strands of black leather, thinking that's what her tendons and muscles were doing right now, knotting up.

Chase might be a better driver than she was, but she'd be uneasy riding with someone who was known for speed and aggressiveness behind the wheel.

"You'd rather go in a Honda Civic than a Corvette?"

Swallowing her pride, she opted for honesty. "I've got to tell you, Chase, I'm not comfortable riding in that car."

"Not even with me driving?" he asked.

*Especially* with him driving.

"Would you mind if I followed you in my car?" she asked.

His brow wrinkled as he studied her expression. "Are you kidding?"

She wished she was.

He placed his hand along her cheek, and she assumed he was going to give in. "I'll tell you what. I promise not to drive over the speed limit. Are you okay with that?"

Not really, but she didn't want to be a slave to her fears. So ignoring her pride, as well as her apprehension, she gave in.

It was tough, though. Tougher than she'd expected.

And for the next half hour, she sat in the passenger seat of his sports car, gripping the armrest, her body tensed as she swayed with each turn in the road.

She wondered if she'd be able to trust her knees to hold her up when they finally arrived. But true to his word, Chase stayed under the speed limit; she knew because she'd been watching the speedometer like a cornered mouse kept its eye on a hawk.

"You've been hanging on to that door ever since I backed out of your driveway," Chase said. "Are you that uncomfortable riding with me?"

She bit her lip and looked away. She wanted to gloss over her fear, to tell him that she'd gotten over the tragedy. And while that was what she'd been telling herself for years, she had to admit that she still carried a few invisible scars. "Ever since the accident, I don't like riding in vehicles, although I do it whenever I have to."

"Like now?" he asked.

She nodded.

"Did you ever get any counseling?"

"No, although I probably needed it at the time."

"Why didn't you?"

"After the accident, I went to live with my grandparents, who were too wrapped up in their own pain to consider therapy for me, or even for themselves."

It had been an awful year. Molly had given up cheerleading and the many friends she'd had when she moved in with her grandparents, which might have been difficult for any other teenager, but at that point, nothing much mattered to her anymore. She'd been too numb to care.

"So you had to deal with it on your own?"

"Yes, and to make it worse, a couple of days later I was almost in another accident."

"What happened?"

"After the funerals, my grandparents took me home to San Antonio to live, and we had to drive. The trip was two hours away, and I followed behind them in the family pickup. But I was on edge the entire time."

"I can understand that," he said.

She was glad that he could, so she continued. "About halfway home, a deer ran across the highway, and my grandfather had to swerve to avoid it. My heart jumped into my throat, and the adrenaline nearly froze in my veins. I hit my brakes, spun out and narrowly missed running off the road. So that experience made things worse."

She didn't tell him that, for a while, she'd had panic attacks each time she'd climbed into a car. It had been years since the last one, though, so she seemed to have overcome them on her own.

"Accidents happen," Chase said. "But I want you to know that I never take risks just for the hell of it. My reactions are keen and quick. I'm always ready for the unexpected—I have to be."

"I'm sure you are. But this isn't about you. It's about me."

He reached over and placed a hand on her knee, warming her from the inside out. "Molly, you're a lot safer riding on city streets with me behind the wheel."

She suspected he might be right, but that didn't make the uneasiness disappear.

But enough of that, she told herself. She had to stop

stressing and get control of herself. And one way to do that was to think—and *talk*—about something else.

She'd decided to attend the Mayfields' party so she could get to know Chase and his family better.

"Tell me about your parents, about your brothers. I'd like to know who I'll be meeting this afternoon."

"There's not much to tell. My dad's name is Phil, and he's retired. He's had some health problems recently and is on dialysis."

"I'm sorry to hear that."

"It's been tough. My brothers and I have all offered to donate a kidney, but my mom insisted that she be the one. That is, if the doctors decide that he's a good candidate for a transplant. We're just waiting to hear."

"It sounds as though your parents have a good relationship," she said.

"As far as I'm concerned, theirs is one of the best. They've always been a team when it comes to parenting us boys, and they made sure to maintain date nights while we were growing up. In fact, they still do."

"Do your brothers have good marriages, too?" she asked.

"Yep. Phillip is an electrical engineer married to Callie, who's a schoolteacher. They have two little girls, which pleases my mom to no end. She never did get to buy dolls or make dresses and frilly things, so now she's in her element."

"Who's next?" Molly asked, realizing that the trees and fence posts were zipping past her window, that her grip on the door handle had loosened, that her ploy was working.

"Bobby is almost two years younger than Phillip. He works on an oil rig outside of Dallas. His wife, Jana, was a beautician, but she's a stay-at-home mom these days. She and Bobby have twin boys, so their lives are involved with Little League and scouting— that sort of thing." Chase turned on his blinker and moments later made a left turn onto a county road. "Last but not least is Danny, who came along two years later. He's in the air force. He and his wife, Susan, just got home from China, where they adopted a little girl."

Wouldn't the "last but not least" refer to Chase? she wondered.

"Are you the baby of the family?" she asked.

"Yeah." His smile seemed to fade, although she suspected it was because he was watching the road, looking for a turnoff. "I came along five years after Danny was born, when my mom and dad thought their family was complete."

Molly placed her hand on her tummy, thinking that surprise babies might be the biggest blessings of all.

"Four boys," she said. "I'll bet your mother deserved a medal."

"I'm sure she'd agree with you. I certainly didn't make things easy for her."

"Why do you say that?"

"Because my brothers were pretty active, and I was determined to not only keep up with them, but to surpass them. As a result, I got more than my share of bruises, stitches and broken bones while I was growing up."

"Your poor mother."

"You've got that right." He chuckled. "And to make matters worse, I considered each one of my injuries a badge of honor."

Molly couldn't imagine what it was like growing up in a family of boys. In fact, at times, she even forgot what her own childhood had been like before the accident, before her parents and brother had died.

Shutting out the memories, the good along with the bad, had helped her deal with her loss over the years. And so had focusing on her work, on her nursing career.

But now that she was pregnant, she realized it might be in the baby's best interest if she tried a little harder to remember the good times.

She glanced across the console at the father of her unborn child and tried to imagine him as a little boy, doing his best to keep up with his older brothers. But she also wondered what kind of father he'd make.

And how he would react when she told him she was having his baby.

Phil and Sandy Mayfield lived on a quiet, tree-lined street in Garnerville, a small suburb north of Houston. As Chase drove through the shady, family-oriented neighborhood, Molly couldn't help thinking it would be a great place in which to raise kids.

Two little girls Rollerbladed down the sidewalk, and several houses down, a boy played with a German shepherd puppy on the lawn.

Chase pulled along the curb and parked in front of a white, single-story home that had a basketball hoop over the garage door and a small wrought-iron table and chair on the porch.

As Molly climbed from the passenger seat, she was glad to be able to keep her legs steady, that she hadn't suffered any ill effects from the stressful drive out here.

"Have your parents lived here long?" she asked.

"We moved here right before I started kindergarten." Chase clicked on the remote lock, then placed a hand on her lower back as he guided her to the walkway that led to the stoop, where a woven, heart-shaped mat welcomed visitors.

Chase had no more than turned the knob when the door swung open. They were met by a middle-aged redhead wearing a pair of black jeans and a pale yellow sweatshirt with a mama duck and a couple of ducklings on the front.

She greeted Chase with a dimpled smile and a hug before turning to Molly and extending a hand. "I'm Sandy Mayfield. You must be Molly. I'm so glad you could make it."

Molly smiled, greeting the woman warmly. "It's nice to meet you."

"Where's the birthday boy?" Chase asked, scanning the living room, apparently looking for his father.

"He's with Phillip and Callie. We're trying to surprise him, so they took him to that new Home Depot down on Main and Third Street. They're going to keep him out of the house until four."

"Who else is here?" Chase asked.

"Danny and Susan, but they took the baby for a walk. They'll be back shortly." Sandy reached for a gold-framed picture on the table in the entry. "Here's a photograph of Amy. We took it right after she arrived. Isn't she the cutest thing? She reminds me of a little doll."

"She's beautiful," Molly said, looking at the photo of a baby girl who appeared to be about nine to twelve months old.

"Jana went to pick up the cake for me," Sandy said, as she replaced the photograph. "She left Bobby and the boys here. They're in the backyard."

"What are they doing?" Chase asked.

"Playing football, I think. And your grandmother is watching them." Sandy nodded over her shoulder. "Why don't you take Molly out and introduce her?"

"All right, I will." Chase led Molly through the kitchen and out a sliding glass door.

The football game stalled when a man bearing a slight resemblance to Garth Brooks noticed Chase and made a time-out motion with his hands.

The men greeted each other with a hug, and Chase introduced Molly to his older brother. After they'd made the customary small talk, Bobby called over his boys, Brandon and Todd, to meet her.

Chase certainly had a large family, and half of them had yet to arrive. Molly wondered if she'd ever be able to keep the names straight.

"Don't forget about me," a silver-haired woman called out.

"No way, Grandma. I'd never do that." Chase took Molly to meet Ellen Mayfield, an attractive woman in her late seventies, who sat in one of several lawn chairs that had been set up for guests.

The game resumed, and moments later the football spiraled toward the women. Chase snatched it in the air, then joined his brother and the boys on the lawn.

"Have a seat," Ellen said, indicating a chair next to her, and Molly complied.

"So you're Chase's girl," the older woman said.

"Actually, we're really just friends." The words, while still hanging in the air, sounded phony, even to Molly, since their friendship seemed to be evolving into something more by the minute.

"Well, it's always nice when one of the boys brings home a friend," the older woman said. "Have you known Chase very long?"

Not long enough, Molly thought, as she considered the baby she was carrying. "A month or two."

"I suppose you're a racing fan."

"Not really."

Ellen smiled and patted Molly's knee. "I'm sure that'll change."

"I doubt it. I prefer a quiet life."

"Well, don't let Chase and his hell-bent-for-leather attitude fool you. He's really a family man at heart."

Molly watched him wrestle one of his nephews to the ground. "I can see that."

"Oh, you mean the rough-and-tumble stuff?" Ellen chuckled and crossed her liver-spotted hands in her lap. "The Mayfield boys are competitive, and Chase is more so than the rest. But one of these days, the right woman will come along, and Chase will settle down and become the man he was always meant to be."

It was clear the older woman was trying to encourage

a match between Molly and Chase, but there was too much against them already—more than she could imagine.

"You know," Ellen added, "I truly believe that there's a master plan, and some things are set in stone."

Molly hoped she wasn't going to suggest that Chase and Molly were made for each other, that they were meant to be a couple. Sure, they might be sexually compatible. And there was a definite attraction, which was important. But that wasn't enough.

"Take Chase, for example." The woman lifted one of her hands and placed it over her brow, blocking out the glare from the afternoon sun as she watched the game playing out on the lawn. "My son and daughter-in-law thought their family was complete, but God had other plans."

Chase had mentioned that he'd been a surprise baby.

"And ever since one of his older brothers referred to him as a family accident, he's been trying to prove otherwise." Ellen sighed. "It was heartbreaking. You should have heard the emotion in his little voice when he came to me with tears welling in his eyes and asked if it was true."

"They were teasing him about it?" Molly asked.

"Yes, and rather unmercifully, if you ask me. But you know how children can be."

Yes, Molly thought. She did know. "What did you say to him?"

"I told him that some of the best gifts were surprises, but I'm not sure if that made him feel better about it. I'd seen the pain flicker in his eyes, the anger."

It made sense to Molly, and her heart swelled at the

thought of the little boy trying his darnedest to prove that he was just as good if not better than anyone else in the family.

As time went on that day, Danny and Susan returned from their walk with little Amy. The newly adopted baby was a beautiful child, with pudgy cheeks, dark tufts of hair and bright little eyes, and Molly couldn't help sharing the couple's obvious joy.

She wondered how her child would fit into this family, and if the two little ones would be close.

Susan pulled up a chair and sat, holding Amy on her lap, while Danny joined the other Mayfield males on the lawn.

The teams were uneven, Molly noted, but it didn't seem to matter.

As she sat on the sidelines, watching the fun-filled one-upmanship between Chase and his siblings, she easily saw where he'd gotten such a competitive nature.

During a halftime lull, Chase ambled toward the women and stooped beside Molly, putting his shoulder next to hers.

"So what do you think so far?" he asked, his breath coming out in short gasps following the effort he'd expended in the football game.

"I think you boys must have driven your poor mother to distraction."

He laughed. "We gave it our best shot."

But it was Molly who was driven to distraction, as she found herself drawn closer and closer to the father of her baby. But before she could give it much thought, before she was tempted to reach out and cup his face,

Sandy opened the sliding door and announced, "He's here! Get ready, everyone!"

A hush fell over the patio, as everyone gathered together and waited for Chase's father to arrive. And when he stepped through the doorway, followed by Phillip, Callie and their girls, everyone yelled, "Surprise!"

Phil Mayfield, a tall, lanky man who was balding, broke into a grin. "Well, would you look at this!"

He was a bit on the pale side, Molly noted, realizing his absence of color probably had something to do with his health issues. But he was a friendly man, and his wife, sons and grandchildren clearly adored him.

She stole a glance at Chase, who stood next to her, surrounded by his family. She supposed she'd have to tell him about her pregnancy one of these days soon.

She just wasn't sure when.

Or how.

## Chapter Ten

While Jana and Callie helped their mother-in-law lay out a spread of food on several card tables that had been set up on the patio, Susan and Molly chatted with Chase's grandmother.

It was nice to see Molly fitting in, although Chase had known she would. Pamela had tried, but she'd been a little too stiff, a little too prim and proper.

As Molly smiled and reached for Amy's little hand, she cooed at the new baby. Chase's heart warmed to see her maternal side, a side Pamela had rarely displayed with his nieces and nephews, even though she'd often worked with charitable organizations that targeted underprivileged children in third-world countries. He'd never been able to figure that out.

His cell phone, which hung at his belt, rang, and

he glanced at the lighted display, noting Gerald Barden's number.

Molly, who'd heard the call come in, looked his way and caught his gaze.

Using hand motions while mouthing the words, he said, "I need to take this. Will you excuse me?"

She nodded.

Chase carried his cell phone into the house, but by the time he found a quiet spot to talk to his biggest and most vocal sponsor, the man had hung up. So he continued into the den, where he took a seat in his father's recliner and returned the call.

When Gerald answered, Chase said, "I'm sorry, but I couldn't get to my phone. What's up?"

"Where the hell have you been? I've been calling your house, but all I get is your recorded voice on that blasted machine. And you haven't been answering your cell, either. What did you do? Take a vacation without telling me?"

Actually, Chase had shut down his phone, wanting to take a break from the world of stock car racing and all that went with it. "Yeah, I took a few days off."

If it had been racing season, which was coming up soon, Chase would have understood Gerald's frustration. As it was, it irritated him to be called on the carpet for no reason. "I didn't know that was part of our agreement, Gerald. The last I heard, I was just supposed to stay out of trouble. And that's what I've been doing."

"I can't complain about that," Gerald said.

"So what's the problem?"

"There's no problem. Not really. I just wanted to let

you know that the article about you and that single mother who's strapped for cash went over well. In fact, I thought it would be a good idea for you to invite her and the kids to the barbecue tomorrow. If you give her a call, I'll send a car for her."

Chase bit back a grumble. He hadn't committed to the barbecue, and he didn't like Gerald making assumptions or demands. But he supposed he'd better not fight too much until Gerald agreed to keep sponsoring him.

Besides, he figured the kids would really enjoy a visit to a ranch. He doubted that they got out that much. "Okay, I'll talk to her about that."

"I also invited the reporter who covered the story."

"Great," Chase said, although his voice hadn't quite relayed the enthusiasm that was contained within the definition of the word.

"What about the woman?" Gerald asked.

Diana? Tommy's mother? "What woman?"

"The one you're dating," Gerald said. "Is she coming, too?"

"Her name is Molly. And I'll invite her."

"Good."

A moment of silence stretched across the line.

"I'm not following you, Gerald. You said it's just a barbecue." The man had hosted quite a few of these events in the past, and they'd all been pleasant get-togethers and well attended. But this one seemed to be different.

"It is just the usual. No big deal. But wear a little something special, will you?"

"What do you mean by *special?*"

"Dress up a bit. Shave. Turn on the old Chase Mayfield charm. That's all I mean."

"All right."

"And tell me about the woman."

"Molly?"

"Yeah, the one you're dating. The nurse. How serious are you?"

Far more serious than Chase had expected to be, but he wasn't sure how much he wanted to reveal to Gerald—and for a multitude of reasons.

"Do you plan on marrying her?" Gerald asked, prodding for the information Chase had held back.

"I'm not sure," he finally said. "Why does it matter?"

"No reason."

There was always a reason for Gerald's questions. And if Chase hadn't thought about asking Molly to marry him, he might have taken issue with it.

Hell, he was taking issue with it anyway.

Everything inside Chase urged him to rebel, but the season was barreling down on him, and he couldn't risk alienating his biggest sponsor.

"Molly and I will be there tomorrow," he said, albeit reluctantly.

He just hoped she didn't balk when he told her it was a command performance.

The birthday celebration had gone off without a hitch. The meal had been tasty, and the German chocolate cake, which was Phil Mayfield's favorite, had been remarkably good.

Molly had sat on the fringe of the party at first, and

while she still didn't have all the names straight, it hadn't taken her long to get into the family spirit. The Mayfields, of course, had a certain number of inside jokes and memories of special times, things she hadn't been a part of, but that was to be expected.

Still, it felt great to be a part of a loving camaraderie again, even if Chase's family was a little over the top in some ways—the competitive edge, for one. But they'd all gone out of their way to be nice to Molly, including her in the conversation, asking her questions about the medical center.

As the party was wearing down, everyone began to pitch in and carry bowls of leftover food and dirty dishes into the house, but Jana quickly chased them off. "If we get too many people in here bumping into each other, it's going to slow the process. Mom, why don't you and Grandma watch the baby for Susan?"

"That's the best chore I've had all day," Sandy Mayfield said as she happily took the baby from Susan's arms and carried her into the living room.

Jana even shooed off Chase, who'd carried in the last bowl from outside. "Help Dad and your brothers get that new LCD TV set up, will you? I know that's what you'd rather be doing. And don't worry about Molly. We're going to take good care of her." Then Jana slipped her arm through Molly's and led her to the kitchen.

It felt good to be accepted, to be one of the girls.

She stood at the sink, her hands in warm soapy water as she washed the dishes. Callie, Phillip's wife, was drying a serving bowl, but after she opened a cupboard door to put it away, her movements stalled. Molly, who was being especially observant, noticed that she seemed to zone out for a while. Then she slowly faced the women in the kitchen, the bowl and dish towel still in her arms. "I haven't told Phillip yet, but I just found out that I'm pregnant."

"Really?" Susan, who'd just adopted Amy, brightened and stepped closer. "Congratulations! Maybe the girls will get a brother this time."

"Thanks," Callie said, although her attempt to smile failed miserably. "It's just that… Well, we weren't planning on a third child. I just got a promotion at work, and now…"

Jana sidled up to Callie and wrapped an arm around her waist. "This baby is going to be a wonderful addition to the family. And you'll be happy, once you get used to the idea."

"I'm sure you're right." Callie took a fortifying breath, then slowly let it out. "But twelve years ago, when the girls were babies, we didn't have a mortgage to worry about. And now that we do, it means I won't be able to stay at home this time. And we'll have to put the poor kid in day care as an infant."

Molly had yet to consider that problem. What would she do with her baby when her maternity leave ran out? When she had to go to work to support both of them?

"Everything will work out," Jana said. "It always does."

Molly watched the women rally, thinking it would be nice to be a part of something like that.

"I could watch the baby for you," Susan said. "Now that we have Amy, I'm not working. And it'll be nice for the cousins to be close."

Relief washed across Callie's face. "Thanks. I'd feel so much better leaving a newborn with someone I know."

Susan smiled. "So, now that we've got that problem solved, what else can we help you with?"

Callie's eyes filled with tears. "You guys are the best. I never had sisters, so having you is a real treat."

"I know what you mean," Jana said, chuckling. "Living with a Mayfield man isn't easy, but at least you and Susan have daughters to take the edge off all that testosterone."

"Be careful," Callie warned her sisters-in-law. "We'll scare off Molly."

All three of the women turned toward the sink, where Molly stood. Smiles lit their faces, as they included her yet again.

But she wasn't scared.

Not yet.

"Of course," Jana said, crossing her arms, "Molly has the toughest Mayfield of all to deal with."

Something told her there was a world of truth in that statement, and an uneasiness began to settle over her for the first time since she'd arrived.

"At least Chase zeroed in on a nurse this time," Jana said, chuckling. "Now he'll have his own private medical professional to tend to him."

Molly's heart dropped to the pit of her stomach, as the meaning of Jana's words rang out.

"But I predict a change coming down the pike," Callie said. "Did you see the way he was looking at her all evening? That boy has it bad."

Molly didn't know about that, but it did seem likely

that Chase was thinking about settling down, which was probably why he'd wanted her to meet his family. And while she'd agreed to come with him, it was more out of curiosity, since these people would be her baby's relatives.

Still, she'd been lowering her guard all day, getting to know the Mayfields—and liking them more than she'd expected.

But maybe Callie was right. It was possible that Chase was getting ready to make some big changes in his life. And if so, then Molly might be able to commit to him after all.

He hadn't come right out and said anything about marriage. But if he did bring it up, she'd have to give the idea some careful consideration.

Molly wasn't the kind of person who placed demands on other people, and if Chase's hobby or occupation was anything else, anything safe, she wouldn't dream of asking him to give it up. But racing stock cars was dangerous. Even his sisters-in-law knew it.

So if their relationship stood any chance, Molly would have do something she hadn't planned or wanted to do before.

She would have to give Chase an ultimatum.

On the way home, Chase noticed that Molly wasn't sitting quite as stiffly as she'd been on the drive to his parents' house. But she wasn't completely relaxed, either.

Had he pushed his family on her too soon in their relationship?

Or was she still worried about his driving?

Maybe she was stressing about what would happen

once they got home. Was she giving any thought to sleeping with him again?

Chase really wanted to spend the night with her, but maybe she wasn't ready.

"Did you have fun tonight?" he asked.

She turned and looked across the console at him. "Yes, I really enjoyed myself. You have a great family. And they were very nice to me."

"That's not surprising."

"Well, it surprised me a bit."

"Why?"

She glanced down to her lap, at her hands, which rested on her knees. "Because I'm nothing like your ex."

No, she wasn't, which was one of the many things that had drawn him to Molly in the first place. Yet Pamela's name hadn't really come up in their conversations in the past, so he wondered how Molly had heard about her.

He figured someone at the party must have mentioned her, which was okay. The divorce was no secret.

But did Molly feel uneasy about the other woman? Did she wonder if she would measure up? If so, he'd have to put her mind at ease.

"For what it's worth, Pamela never really found her niche in the family. In fact, sometimes after a get-together like we had today, she'd complain on the way home."

"About what?"

"About no one even trying a bite of her liver pâté and how they all seemed to wolf down Callie's chips and salsa fresca." He again glanced across the seat at Molly, saw that she was staring straight ahead. Yet in the moonlight, he spotted a faint smile.

"Pamela was a little too cosmopolitan," he added for clarification, "and a little too stuffy for the Mayfield clan."

"Really? With all her charity work, I'd think that she was more down to earth than that."

Pamela might have supported third-world charities, but her efforts supplied the funds for others to make the trips. She'd never wanted to go herself.

He wasn't sure how to explain it to Molly without making his ex-wife out to be a bad guy, which some divorced people might do. But he didn't think that was an entirely fair assessment of the woman.

"I don't mean to imply that Pamela's not a nice person," he went on to say. "She was brought up in a wealthy home, but she's not spoiled or snooty. I think you'd probably like her if you met her."

"I seriously doubt that'll happen."

Well, if Molly went to the Bardens' ranch with him tomorrow, she might have the chance to meet Pamela in the flesh. Not that he'd feel especially comfortable with that. But Gerald was his sponsor, and they were looking forward to another successful racing season. Consequently, there were a few things that just couldn't be helped.

Chase stole another glance at Molly and saw that her smile had become more defined.

That was a good sign, he decided. Maybe it was time to spring the barbecue on her.

"What are you doing tomorrow?" he asked.

"Laundry for one thing. Grocery shopping, too."

"Can you do that in the morning?"

"I suppose I can. Why?"

"My sponsors are having a little get-together at the ranch one of them owns. We had a good season last year, so it's kind of a celebration." He didn't mention that it had become an annual thing, where they kicked off the upcoming season, as well.

Gerald could always throw a wrench into the machinery and refuse to sponsor Chase again, although that wasn't likely. Especially when he got a chance to meet Molly.

"It should be fun. And I can guarantee that the food will be delicious."

She didn't respond, so he added, "In fact, they invited Diana Haines and her kids to go."

"That's really nice." Molly turned in her seat, facing him for a change, rather than gripping the door. "Where's the ranch?"

"Not far from Brighton Valley."

Okay, so he was stretching the truth a bit. Barden's ranch was at least forty miles from Molly's house, but he didn't want to give her any reason to turn him down.

He continued to look at the road ahead, but he couldn't help wondering what she was doing, what she was thinking.

Finally, she said, "I'll think about it, okay?"

"Great." He couldn't help feeling as though he'd just won the Braxton 500, even though she hadn't come out and said yes.

He'd no more than turned his gaze back to the road ahead when a young coyote darted across his field of vision, only to stop and freeze in the headlights.

Instinctively, he swerved to avoid making roadkill of

the critter, and Molly let out a half gasp, half scream, which startled the bejeezus out of him and made him wonder if he'd missed seeing something a lot worse than the animal.

When he'd righted the car, he glanced her way.

Her hand covered her chest, and her eyes were closed as she struggled to catch her breath.

"Don't worry," he said. "I missed it."

She didn't respond.

"Accidents happen," he said, "but I'm good at avoiding them."

"How can you be sure?" she asked. "Someday your reflexes might not be as quick."

Now probably wasn't the time to discuss her fears, with her clearly gripping the door handle again and ready to eject right out of the sunroof. He wanted to be sensitive, but he also wanted to help her. He just didn't know how to go about it.

He let the subject drop for a few minutes, then, deciding to get her mind off the road, which had suddenly become even more of a focus than it had before, he said, "That little Amy sure is a sweetheart."

By bringing up his family again, a diversionary ploy that had worked before, he hoped to wade through some of the tension that had built inside the car.

"She's a beautiful child," Molly said. "Susan told me that she and Bobby just returned from China with her a month or so ago."

"They were there for several weeks. You'd be surprised at how much paperwork and red tape there is to deal with."

They chatted about his dad's dialysis, as well as his grandmother's upcoming move to Garnerville so she would be closer to his parents. And by the time they hit the Brighton Valley city limits, Molly had settled back into her seat again.

Chase could understand her nervousness, at least to an extent. He just couldn't figure out why she wouldn't trust his driving, why she couldn't trust him to look out for her safety.

Sure, she'd told him about the accident in which she'd lost her parents, but he was a professional driver. And he had quick reactions.

When they parked in front of Molly's house, Mrs. Carlisle, the elderly neighbor who lived across the street, was trying to drag a trash can from the garage to the curb and not having much success.

"Wanda," Molly called, as she climbed from the car. "Let me get that for you."

Chase jumped out of the car and jogged across the street. "I've got it, ladies."

As he carried the can down the drive and to the curb, he heard Molly chatting with the elderly woman.

"You're limping, Wanda. Is that knee bothering you again?"

"It always bothers me a little, but I've got an ingrown toenail that hurts like old fury. I'm wearing bedroom slippers, but the fool thing is still giving me fits."

"Do you want me to take a look at it?" Molly asked.

"Heavens, no. Not when your young man is here. I'll let you check on it tomorrow. And if you think I ought to make a doctor's appointment, I'll give his office a call on Monday morning."

Wanda glanced down the drive and spotted her trash can, then she looked at Chase and smiled. "I sure appreciate that, young man."

"My pleasure."

"Well, I'll let you kids get after it." Then she turned and half hopped, half shuffled up the drive and into the garage. She paused near the entry to the house long enough to push the button to the automatic door opener, lowering it and securing herself in for the night.

"She was really limping," Chase said.

"I know. I worry about her sometimes."

Chase didn't mention that Wanda worried about Molly, too. But he found it kind of cute. That's what neighbors were for, he supposed.

He walked with Molly up to the porch, wondering if she'd invite him in. He didn't dare wonder about anything more than that right now.

"Thanks for coming with me today," he said.

"I had a good time."

He'd told Gerald that he would bring her to the barbecue, and he was glad he had. He still wasn't sure how to help her work through her fear, but he hoped that the more she got out, the more she became a part of his world, the easier it would be for her.

"I thought I'd pick you up about one," he said, going out on a limb. "If that's okay." She'd implied that she would go with him. Or at least, she hadn't said no. But that was before the damn coyote ran into the street, which might have set her back.

"Look, I'll go with you, but would you mind if I met you there?"

He guessed that the near-miss had caused her fears to kick into high gear after all.

Or did she not want to look like a couple when they arrived?

Either way, he decided to push a little.

"It would really mean a lot to me if you'd let me pick you up."

She hesitated, clearly still rattled by the incident with the coyote. "Okay. I'll go."

Obviously, she wasn't going to invite him in. But he wasn't going to push about that. Instead, he gave her another one of those slow, memorable kisses that had set her on fire the last time they'd been together.

"You're going to invite me inside again one day," he said. "And when you do, I'm going to make you glad you did."

"Oh, yeah?" she said, a grin tickling her lips.

"You can count on it."

Then he turned and headed back to his car. For a moment, he questioned the certainty in his words.

Maybe because that kiss they'd shared had been lacking something.

The spark that had been in their first kiss, he decided. And the innocent longing that had been in the second.

On his way to the car, he hoped against hope that she would call him back. And when she didn't, regret filled his lungs.

He wanted to take one last glance over his shoulder,

to see if she was having second thoughts, but refused to run the risk of seeing that she'd gone inside.

As Chase ambled down the walk, preparing to get into his car, Molly stood on the porch and watched him go, her lips still tingling from his kiss.

"Chase," she said, calling after him.

When he turned, she didn't remain rooted in one spot, expecting him to come to her. She met him halfway.

He seemed to understand all she struggled with, because he placed his hand on her cheek, whisked his thumb across her skin and gazed into her eyes. "What's the matter?"

"I'd like you to stay. I mean, if you want to."

A smile stole across his face. "I do. But are you sure?"

She'd been uncertain about a lot of things since meeting him, but not about her attraction to him, her desire for him. "I definitely want you to stay. But the rest...the rest is complicated."

"I'm sure we can sort it all out if we put our heads together."

There it was again, his agreement to find some middle ground on an issue that was tearing her apart. His smile convinced her that working it out might be a lot easier than she'd imagined.

"I'd like that." Then she took him by the hand and led him into the house, where Rusty met them in the entry with an I'm-hungry/Where-have-you-been? meow.

After greeting and feeding the cat, Molly secured the front door. Then she and Chase retired to the bedroom, which was lit by soft lamplight.

"I shouldn't feel so awkward," she said.

"No, you shouldn't." His gaze locked on hers, and she let go of her apprehension, reminding herself how badly she wanted him, wanted this. How nothing else mattered. How they'd work everything out.

They both undressed slowly and deliberately, their eyes on each other the entire time.

When they'd set aside their clothing, she turned back the comforter and they climbed into bed and came together like lovers who'd grown comfortable with each other over the years.

As Chase slipped his arms around her, drawing her close, he placed his lips on hers in a warm, blood-stirring kiss.

And with each heated touch, each arousing caress, each hungry kiss, Molly shut out her worries, amazed at how good they were together and telling herself that nothing else mattered.

When they reached a peak, they climaxed together and rode each ebb and flow until they lay completely spent.

Chase's ragged breathing lulled her, and as she closed her eyes, she let go of almost everything that held her back. Yet she didn't let go of him, didn't turn away.

Instead, she held on to Chase as though she could make the moment last forever.

And she sure hoped she could.

Because she'd fallen in love with Chase Mayfield, even though she was afraid to let him know.

## Chapter Eleven

In spite of Molly's secrets—her feelings for Chase and the baby they'd conceived—she slept better that night than she had in ages.

Of course, being cradled in Chase's arms had surely helped.

The next morning, after they showered and dressed, Chase insisted upon fixing her a breakfast of pancakes, orange juice and coffee. For a moment she suffered a wave of nausea, excused herself and hurried to the bathroom. But after a few minutes of slow breathing, it passed.

Now, as they sat at the table, she studied the man across from her, his hair damp and mussed. Even the scar over his brow added a rugged edge to his handsome face.

She couldn't believe her luck in finding him, and her heart swelled.

"I thought we'd leave for the barbecue around ten," he said. "Is that okay with you?"

"I guess so." She'd really prefer to meet him there, but if their relationship was going to develop into something special, something lasting, they would have to go places together—and in the same car. So she supposed she'd have to get used to letting Chase drive once in a while.

"I'm not sure if Pamela will be there," he added, "but there's a good possibility that she'll show up. So I wanted to give you a heads-up."

Molly wasn't keen on meeting his ex-wife, although that didn't mean she wouldn't like to check her out from a distance. "I'm all right with that. But why is she going to be there?"

"Because her father is my biggest sponsor."

Somehow, that bit of news didn't sit well. Molly didn't like thinking that Chase was still locked in with his ex, with his past. But she was an adult, and so was Pamela.

Besides, from what Molly understood, the barbecue was an end-of-the-season wrap-up. And she was hoping that Chase would use it as a springboard to announce his retirement. After all, he knew how she felt about racing, and he'd said they could reach a compromise. What else could he have possibly meant?

So that being the case, she would make every effort to attend and support him, even if that meant strapping herself into the passenger seat of his new sports car and putting her life in his hands.

Now that was certainly a compromise.

"Where's the ranch?" she asked.

"About thirty or forty miles north of Brighton Valley, but it's an easy drive."

It didn't sound like an easy drive to Molly, but she tried not to think about it. She'd made it through Saturday, as well as that fearful moment when the coyote had run onto the road.

Besides, after meeting Chase's family, she'd begun to feel better about being involved with him. And sleeping together again last night had made their bond stronger.

She was beginning to think they had a chance to be a real couple, one with a bright future.

Chase had told her he'd been staying at the Brighton Valley Motor Inn, so he needed to go back so he could shave and get a change of clothing.

She supposed she could have told him to bring his things back with him, but she wasn't quite ready for a move like that, although she could be soon. It depended a lot on whether he indicated some plan to give up racing in the not-too-distant future.

"I'll be back by ten," he told her before giving her a kiss goodbye.

She planned to use the time to fix her hair and put on her makeup. She'd also need to find something special to wear. She'd chosen her newest pair of jeans and a white cotton blouse, the closest thing she had to western wear, which she thought would be appropriate for a barbecue at a ranch.

While she was applying mascara, the finishing touch, the doorbell rang.

"Just a minute," she called out, thinking Chase might have forgotten something.

When she answered, she found Wanda on the porch wearing her housecoat and slippers.

"I waited until after Chase left," the elderly woman said. "Did you want to look at my toe now?"

"Of course, come on inside."

Wanda entered the house slowly, then took a seat on the sofa. As she carefully removed her slipper, she winced and blew out a labored little huff.

Molly drew closer. She couldn't help but frown when she spotted the woman's big toe, which was terribly swollen. The red, angry flesh was clearly infected.

She couldn't be sure, but she thought the start of a red streak had formed, indicating that Wanda might have blood poisoning.

"This needs to be treated," she told the woman. "And it can't wait until tomorrow. You're going to have to go to the E.R. today."

"There goes the entire morning," Wanda said. "That place is a zoo on the weekends. And the wait is going to be awful."

Molly couldn't argue about that.

"My doctor's office opens at eight tomorrow morning," Wanda said, "so maybe if I'm there when they open the door, they'll fit me in first thing."

That wasn't a good idea. Molly straightened and watched as the woman struggled to replace the slipper on her foot. "I'll tell you what, Wanda. I'll drive you to Urgent Care. The wait shouldn't be too long."

"Gosh, I hate to have you do that."

"I really don't mind." In fact, there was a part of Molly that welcomed an excuse to arrive late at the barbecue. And to drive her own car. "Give me a minute, though. All right?"

There'd been several reasons Molly had wanted to drive out to the ranch. But none of them were as believable and as commendable as the excuse that had just fallen in her lap.

While Wanda waited, Molly called Information and requested the phone number of the Brighton Valley Motor Inn. She called and, when someone answered, she asked to speak to Mr. Mayfield's room.

Chase answered on the second ring.

"It's Molly," she said. "I have to take Wanda to see a doctor. Her toe is very badly infected, so I'm going to have to meet you at the ranch. I'll get there as soon as I can."

He paused a beat, as though pondering her words. Or maybe he was contemplating an argument.

Instead, he asked, "You're not going to blow it off, are you?"

Apparently, Chase had yet to learn that when Molly said she would do something, she did it. "Believe it or not, I'm a woman of my word. I'll be there, Chase."

"I believe it." Then he gave her directions and an address.

To be on the safe side, Molly went to the den, sat at the computer and checked the address on MapQuest.

"Wow," she said, as she studied the screen. She hadn't expected the Barden ranch to be so far off the beaten path. Or that she'd have to take so many unfamiliar roads.

She sat back in the desk chair and sighed. Well, there

was no getting around it. Wanda needed someone with her, and Molly was all she had.

She printed out the instructions, then shut down the computer and grabbed her purse.

"I'm ready now." She waited for Wanda to get slowly to her feet and limp to the door, wincing with each step she took.

In spite of Wanda's discomfort and the inconvenience of spending time in the waiting room of Urgent Care, Molly was glad she had an excuse to drive herself to the ranch.

To be honest, it was just better this way.

As Chase hung up the telephone, he blew out a sigh. He hadn't expected Molly to call and change the game plan. And even though he knew Wanda had a bad toe and he believed the story he'd been given, he couldn't help thinking that Molly was glad that she'd been able to avoid riding with him to the barbecue.

If so, they had more to work on than he'd thought.

Yes, he realized. *They* had work to do, because he meant to be a part of Molly's life, and her problems would be his problems.

He couldn't believe how disappointed he was to be going alone, though. How weird was that? For years he'd been attending functions by himself. But this was different. He'd been looking forward to taking Molly with him, to being a couple, to introducing her to his racing world. And he'd wanted to show her off, as well.

Besides, Gerald was expecting to meet her.

He wondered what his sponsor would say when they

didn't arrive together, then he uttered a curse under his breath, irked that he even gave a damn what the man thought. It might have mattered when he'd been married to Pamela, but he and Gerald didn't have that kind of relationship anymore.

Of course, they had the race car connection. And the car was fine-tuned and raring to go once the season started. So after slipping on his boots and grabbing his jacket, he drove the forty miles to Barden's place, a sixty-plus-acre spread considered a gentleman's ranch, where Gerald's friends often gathered to hunt, fish and relax.

The immediate grounds had been set up with rented chairs and tables, complete with linen coverings and flower arrangements.

Just to the left of the place where a buffet line had been set up, a trailer had been parked with Chase's stock car prominently displayed, washed, waxed and ready to go.

Dark clouds gathered on the horizon, and he wondered if Gerald was prepared for rain. Probably, if Pamela had anything to do with the planning.

He'd no more than climbed out of his new Corvette when Gerald came up to greet him. "Chase. It's good to see you. But where's your lady friend?"

"She's going to meet me here. She had to drive one of her neighbors to the doctor, so hopefully that won't take too long."

"Good. Come with me. There are a few people in the house that I want you to meet."

For some reason, Chase always felt as though he was

on display whenever he and Gerald were together, but he'd gotten used to it over the years.

As they reached the veranda, Gerald said, "I sent my foreman to Brighton Valley to pick up Mrs. Haines and her kids. They ought to be here any minute."

"Who's inside?" he asked.

"Herb Eubanks, a guy who'd like to offer you a couple of endorsements. And he's got a few other things to bring to the table."

As Chase strode next to Gerald on their way to the house, a white van with *KRHA News* painted along the side pulled up and parked near the stock car.

"What's with the dog and pony show?" Chase asked.

"It's not a show. Not exactly. Think of it as the public seeing a day in the life of Chase Mayfield, stock car driver and all 'round good guy. I'm doing my best to put you in a good light, son, and I think you ought to appreciate that."

The business part of it was fine. Chase didn't mind talking endorsements and money. But he didn't like Gerald thinking that he was a part of some kind of wacky reality show.

They climbed up the steps to the front door. As they entered the sprawling ranch house, Pamela greeted them. She had some color to her face these days, but what really caught his attention was the way her black top stretched over an obvious baby bump.

As Gerald continued on, Chase and Pamela greeted each other with a kiss on the cheek, a stiff and awkward display that told the world they were adults who'd gotten over whatever issues had led to their divorce.

"When's the baby due?" Chase asked.

"In October."

"Congratulations."

"Thanks." She smiled and caressed her tummy. "It's a boy, so Daddy, of course, is thrilled."

Chase imagined that he was. Gerald adored "Pammy" but he was a man's man and had always wanted a son who'd hunt and fish with him. Maybe that's why Chase had fit the bill and why Gerald continued to keep him around.

When he'd been married to Pamela, Chase had liked the paternal attention he'd gotten, the attention he hadn't needed to share or fight for. Hell, even when he'd offered to give up one of his kidneys for his father, he'd somehow ended up last on the list of possible donors. So the pseudo father-son relationship with Gerald had worked out for both of them.

Lately, though, it didn't seem to be working quite as well as it once had.

About ten minutes later, after Chase had been introduced to Herb Eubanks and played the endorsement courting game, Diana Haines and her kids arrived at the ranch.

"You're going to have to excuse me," Chase said, jumping on the chance to slip away from the formal stuff.

Once outside, he approached Diana and the kids. "Hey, you made it."

"Yeah," Tommy said. "I never got to see a real ranch before."

Well, Gerald Barden's place wasn't a working ranch—it was more for show than anything, but Chase kept that to himself.

"Is that your race car?" Tommy asked, his good arm outstretched and pointing at the trailer.

"Yep. Do you want to check it out?"

"I sure do. Cool."

As they walked toward the car, a news crew and the reporter joined them.

It was nice to see Tommy happy, but the boy and his family had clearly been set up. Used.

A knot formed in Chase's gut as he realized that he'd been a part of it, but he didn't know how to make things right at this point.

When they reached the car, Chase checked it over carefully. The body work had been completed, which had repaired the dents and scrapes it had gotten during the last race.

It had never looked better, he decided. And he looked forward to climbing behind the wheel again, to hearing the engine roar to life.

"Why don't we let Tommy sit in the car," the cameraman said.

That ought to give the guys from the news station the human-interest story and the pictures they'd driven out here to get. So maybe they'd be on their way before too long.

As a man lifted the boy and let him slide through the window into the car, Diana grinned from ear to ear.

A camera flashed, and Chase's gut knotted tighter.

"Can I sit in it next?" Tommy's little sister asked, clapping her hands and hopping up and down.

Apparently, everyone was happy, so Chase didn't know why he was letting it bother him.

Maybe because he was a far cry from being happy about any of it. In fact, he felt at loose ends—as if something was missing. And it, or rather *she,* was.

What in the hell was keeping Molly?

About the time he'd begun to wonder if she was going to show up at all, he spotted her car coming down the drive. Too bad he was on the far side of the soon-to-be-open buffet line. He'd have to hike quite a ways to reach her.

He started in that direction, only to see Pamela reach her first.


By the time Molly parked, took a moment to collect herself after the long drive and climbed from the car, her blouse was wrinkled from the seat belt, and perspiration had dampened her underarms.

The visit to Urgent Care hadn't taken much longer than an hour once they'd been called inside. The doctor had agreed that it was a good thing Wanda had come in. After he'd cut into the toe and treated it, he'd given her an injection. Then he'd written out a couple of prescriptions that Molly had taken to the pharmacy.

After dropping Wanda off at home and making sure she was comfortable, Molly had driven to the ranch. But she'd had to stop twice and ask for directions, so she'd arrived later than she'd intended.

The first person to greet her was an obviously pregnant brunette, who reached out her hand. "Welcome to the Circle B Ranch. You must be Molly, Chase's friend. I'm Pamela Barden-Jones."

Molly recognized Chase's ex-wife from the pictures she'd seen in the society section of the newspaper. "I'm sorry I'm late."

"We haven't eaten yet," Pamela said, as she walked her toward the tables where the guests had gathered. "You haven't missed much."

Molly scanned the grounds in search of Chase.

"He's talking to the reporters." Pamela pointed to where a shiny blue race car was on display.

Several people stood near it, looking it over with smiles. A video camera was rolling, and a boy waved from the driver's window, his arm covered with a red cast.

"I was told this was just a little barbecue," Molly said, "but it looks like quite a party." And a major photo op.

"You know Chase," Pamela said.

Actually, right this moment, Molly wasn't sure if she knew him at all.

"Chase downplays things a lot. And then there's my father." Pamela laughed. "Daddy usually throws a big party to kick off the racing season with a little pizzazz. But he went all out this year."

*Kicking off* the new season?

Somehow, Molly had gotten the impression that this was an end-of-the-season celebration.

Pamela's steps slowed and she placed a hand on her distended womb. "Ooh. This kid is bound to be a soccer player. I swear, even if I hadn't had an ultrasound, I would know this baby is a boy. I guess he's eager to get out and join the party."

"When are you due?" Molly asked.

"Next month, and I'll be happy when it's all over."

She rubbed her belly a moment, then began the walk toward the tables again.

"Has your pregnancy been difficult?"

"No, not really. But I guess I'm not one of those women who enjoys being pregnant."

Molly wondered if she would be one of them. She didn't like the bouts of nausea, but she thought she would enjoy feeling the baby move inside.

Again, she scanned the grounds, looking for Chase, and…speak of the devil…

"Hey," Chase said, as he approached Molly with a smile. "You made it."

Yeah, she had. And she was suddenly wanting to turn around and head home. But she offered him a smile instead.

He slipped an arm around her waist and drew her close, which made her feel marginally better.

"Have you seen Michael?" Pamela asked him.

"He's with a couple of the other guys, watching a ball game on television in the den."

"Thanks."

As Pamela started for the house, Molly said, "It was nice meeting you. Good luck with the baby."

Pamela smiled. "It was great meeting you, too. And thanks."

After she was gone, Chase said, "I was beginning to worry about you."

"I'm sorry I was late."

"That's okay. How was your drive out here? Did you have any problem finding it?"

"I took a couple of wrong turns, but it wasn't too bad."

"Good. I'm glad." He gave her an affectionate hug before heading toward the other guests.

As they neared the people who'd gathered to celebrate the new season, Chase steered Molly toward the first of several tables, introducing her to one man after another, as well as the women they were with. There was no way Molly would remember all of them, but she did her best to be friendly, to make polite conversation.

She had to admit they all seemed nice.

One man, Ralph Collins, said, "It's great to finally meet the little gal who tamed Chase Mayfield."

Molly glanced at Chase and smiled, even though something told her Chase hadn't been tamed at all.

When the introductions were finally over and they were alone, she slipped her arm through his. "You gave me the idea that this was a postseason windup, not a preseason rally."

"Does it matter?" he asked.

"Yes, it does."

"Well, we had a very successful racing schedule last time, and we're hoping for another. And the first race is coming up in the next couple of weeks."

Molly's hands grew clammy, and her tummy shimmied, setting off a wave of nausea. "I thought we were going to compromise."

"We will," he said.

"But you're still planning to race?"

His gaze locked on hers, connecting them in an uncomfortable way. "Of course. Racing is what I do, Molly. It's who I am."

Her steps slowed, and her feet grew as heavy as

chunks of asphalt. She'd never be able to get used to seeing Chase speed around a track, to watching him risk his life. And even if she could handle it, even if she was willing to take the risk or pretend it wasn't there, she couldn't do that to their child.

Chase might like the idea of having a son or daughter. He'd probably even make a good father. But no child should have to lose a parent. And with Chase tearing up the track regularly, there'd always be that possibility.

"We can talk more about this later," he said, as he started to make his way toward a chest-high table that had been set up as a bar.

But as much as Molly willed herself to continue on, to smile and make happy chatter, she could hardly move. She wanted to run to her car, to drive back to Brighton Valley before it got dark.

And the only way to do that was to confront him. To admit that she'd misunderstood him, that she'd made a crazy assumption because she'd wanted to believe it so badly. That either way, she hadn't counted on this.

"Remember when I told you that we didn't have anything in common, that I didn't want to be involved with a stock car racer?"

Chase, who'd slowed his pace to match hers, came to a complete stop. "Yeah, but that was before we made love—"

"You also said that we'd be able to work things out, that you'd be willing to compromise."

*"Compromise?"* he asked. "Or quit racing entirely?"

Quitting was the only compromise she was willing to make. "Chase, I can't support your racing. I can't even watch. I…" She shook her head. "If you're going to race, this isn't going to work."

His eye twitched. "Are you giving me an ultimatum?"

She sighed. "I hadn't meant to, but I can't help it at this point."

He crossed his arms. "You said it would be unfair to ask me to quit."

"You're right. And it's unfair for you to expect me to worry myself sick. I'm sorry, Chase." She swept her hand toward the tables, the happy people talking amongst themselves, the race car that had been parked near the buffet line as a guest of honor. "But I can't be a part of this."

"Can't or *won't?*"

At his harsh tone, Molly turned and headed back to her car. She wasn't sure what she was expecting. More of an argument, she supposed. But much to her disappointment, Chase let her go.

As she slid behind the wheel, she felt a bit uneasy about leaving without eating or saying goodbye to anyone else, but fear and disappointment won out. And so did the heartbreak.

She couldn't stay a minute longer. Besides, it had been tough enough finding her way here. And she had to get closer to Brighton Valley before darkness set in.

She'd gotten no more than ten miles from the ranch when droplets of water began to splatter the windshield.

"Damn." She turned on the wipers, but the steady swoosh-swoosh did little to make her feel comfortable about driving home in the rain.

It's not that she'd never had to drive in bad weather

before, she just hadn't done so very often. Nor for more than a few blocks.

She kept on going, hands on the wheel, eyes peeled ahead, watching for anything that could cause her to lose control of the car.

Ten more miles, she told herself, knowing she'd turn onto a more familiar road then.

Nine miles.

Eight.

If she weren't so nervous, she'd cry. But she couldn't afford to think of Chase right now, to grieve for what she'd lost.

What she'd thrown away.

She hadn't wanted to issue an ultimatum, yet she had. And the unfairness of it struck her. Racing defined him, just as nursing did her. And she'd backed him into a corner.

It wasn't his fault that she'd fallen in love with him. Or that she would worry herself sick when he raced. Or that she was uneasy riding with him.

Uneasy? Was that really it? Or was it stone-cold fear?

No matter what she'd told herself, she *was* still dealing with the accident. And at times, her fear had crippled her.

She didn't want to live like this forever—alone. Afraid.

She only had two options: she could live with Chase or live without him. Either way, the fear would remain in her life until she faced it and addressed it. And the first one who needed to hear her realization was Chase. She also owed him an apology.

But it was too late to do that now.

The windshield wipers continued to swoosh, ticking off the minutes and the miles.

Ahead she spotted the sign that announced the turn she'd been watching for. Moments later she was headed to Brighton Valley, and her grip on the steering wheel finally relaxed. With each mile marker she passed, her mood rose.

But the peace had little to do with getting home and sequestering herself in her house. It had come from her decision to call Chase this evening and tell him she was sorry, that she loved him, that they'd created a child together. And that she was willing to do whatever it took to have a life with him.

That is, if she hadn't destroyed what fragile connection they'd had.

Either way, there were some definite changes coming in her life.

Instead of going straight home, maybe she ought to stop by the medical center and talk to Betsy, who had a friend who was a licensed counselor. Talking it out with a professional might help.

When she reached the four-way stop on Second Street, she braked, looked both ways, then accelerated.

A horn blared. She reached the center of the intersection just as a white pickup came barreling out of the blue and slammed into her, spinning her car around and knocking her head against the window.

Everything hurt—but all she could think of was the baby.

## Chapter Twelve

Chase hated ultimatums.

And he hated to be told what to do. He'd had enough of that crap as a kid, and then from his sponsors.

So he'd turned away from Molly and headed back to the party, back to the people who cared about him.

Or maybe they only cared about what he was able to bring them—victory and an adrenaline rush by proxy.

How could Molly take all they'd had, all he'd wanted to give her, and throw it in his face like that? How could she tell him he had to give up racing or lose her?

When he reached the tables, where the sponsors and their guests had gathered to await the go-ahead to get into the buffet line, Gerald strode up to him.

The fiftysomething man, who stood six foot two and weighed well over two hundred pounds, placed a hand on Chase's shoulder. "Where'd your lady friend take off to?"

"Home, I guess."

"Why? Did you two have a fight?"

Chase didn't respond.

"Well, apparently she's not as crazy about you as you thought."

Chase turned to face the man who'd been like a father to him. "Listen, Gerald. I appreciate all you've done for me. But let it go, will you?"

"I can't. I don't want to see your mind scattered when you need to be focusing on the upcoming season. And I don't want to hear about you nursing a broken heart by carousing late at night and gallivanting with all the little groupies who flock around you."

For some reason, Gerald had a way of making Chase feel like a spoiled little boy who would never grow up, never be completely on his own. And it was getting old.

*Real old.*

Gerald raised his finger in a parental fashion. "Are you listening to me?"

"I heard you," Chase said. "But I'm not taking it to heart. I don't mind you providing me with advice and direction during the racing season. But my private life is a different story."

Gerald stiffened. "Have you forgotten who I am?"

"Who *are* you, Gerald?"

For a moment Chase wondered if the man was going to roll up that index finger and curl his hand into a menacing fist instead. "I'm the guy who made you the driver you are today."

Oh, yeah? Well, Chase had been the one out on the track, choking on smoke and dust and doing what came naturally to him.

And while Gerald had made it possible for him to reach a higher level of racing, he hadn't been all that instrumental.

Chase crossed his arms. "You know, to be honest, my father first spotted my talent when I was a kid. And he worked two jobs to enable me to compete on the junior circuit."

"Your dad wouldn't have been able to afford to buy you a car like mine."

"You're right. But that doesn't mean he wouldn't have wanted to. Or that he wouldn't have tried."

"Then why didn't he?"

The question poked a finger at Chase's chest, daring him to think about things he'd been ignoring for ages. Like why had the wealthy man become a father figure to him? And why had Chase tried so hard to please him?

At first it had been because of Pamela. And when Gerald had taken him under his wing, it had been nice not to have to compete against anyone else for that paternal attention.

Chase's gut clenched. Had he chosen a relationship with Gerald over one with his own father? A relationship in which he was already the top dog and didn't have to try and bump one of his brothers out of the way?

The possibility was unsettling.

And not very admirable.

Chase might have been an unplanned addition to the family, but his parents had cared for him. And he'd found his own place in their hearts, even if he hadn't always thought the niche was good enough.

Maybe his biggest competition had been himself and his need to be bigger, better, faster…

"Come on," Gerald said. "Let's get a plate of food. The buffet's open now."

Chase wasn't hungry. And he definitely wasn't in the mood for a party.

A raindrop splattered on his face, followed by another. He glanced overhead, at the dark clouds that had been steadily moving in. The weather report had said there was only a ten percent chance of precipitation. But they'd obviously miscalculated.

He thought about Molly on the road and tensed, uneasy with her driving in bad weather.

As angry at her as he wanted to be, he couldn't block an onslaught of worry.

She'd told him that she preferred driving over riding, so he'd tried to tell himself that she was probably competent behind the wheel. But she didn't drive very often. Not when she walked or rode her bike to work almost every day.

He remembered how she'd practically clung to the passenger door when they'd gone to his parents' house yesterday, at least for the first hour or so. And how she'd screamed when that fool coyote had run in front of the car.

Maybe she wasn't as competent and as comfortable as she'd wanted him to believe.

And now she was heading home on unfamiliar streets, which would become wet and slick before long.

"Listen, Gerald. I'm not going to stick around for dinner. I need to go."

"But you're the guest of honor, Chase. I can't let you leave now."

"You're going to have to." Chase turned to go, eager to catch up with Molly.

Gerald grabbed his arm, holding him back. "What's that little filly done to you?"

"Nothing," he said. But that wasn't true. Molly had definitely done something to him. She'd burrowed deep into his heart. And right now, he needed to find her, to protect her. To tell her he'd do whatever it took to have her in his life. But none of that concerned Gerald.

Chase pulled his arm free of the older man's grip. "Thanks for the party."

"If you want to drive my car next season, you'll at least stick around until after we eat."

The threat hung in the humidity, but it no longer seemed to matter. Nothing mattered except finding Molly.

"I'm not sure what I want to do next season. But don't threaten me, Gerald. It won't work." Chase reached into his pocket and pulled out his car keys. Then he sprinted toward his Corvette.

Knowing Molly, she'd be driving like a little old lady on her way to an ice cream social, so he had no doubt he'd catch her—if he set his mind to it.

Of course, he had no idea what he'd tell her when he did. Or whether she'd give a squat about anything he had to say.

Hell, what *would* he say? He wasn't sure. He'd

probably start by telling her that he loved her. And that he wanted to work things out—somehow. Because without Molly in his life, the future wouldn't be as bright as it had once seemed.

When he reached the car, he took one last look at the ranch, at the people attending "his" party. People he didn't really know, didn't care to know.

Molly, on the other hand, was the first person who'd gotten beneath his skin, rather than just touching the surface. And he didn't want to lose her.

Once in the car, he started the engine, then took off after her. He wasn't sure if he'd be willing to give up racing for her. But he'd have to seriously consider it.

The rain had begun to sprinkle steadily by the time he saw the Brighton Valley city limits sign. He'd made pretty good time, but he hadn't caught up with her yet.

Minutes later, he spotted an accident up ahead—at the intersection of Second and Main. A white pickup had struck a blue Honda… Oh, God. Was that Molly?

His heart dropped to the pit of his stomach, and fear, the likes of which he'd never felt before, slammed into him. He hit the brakes, shifted into Park and ran toward her car.

Molly sat in the idling vehicle, holding the steering wheel and trying to clear her head. The guy in the pickup was slumped over his dash, so something told her she'd gotten off more easily than he had.

Somebody was going to have to call the paramedics, and she figured it would have to be her.

Her head hurt where she'd bumped it, and her knee

ached. But she was more concerned about the baby. It was so early in her pregnancy; anything could happen. Was it okay? Would she lose it?

Her door swung open, and she turned to look at whoever had come to her aid. She'd planned to tell him or her to check on the other driver first, but when she spotted Chase, his expression clearly panicked, his face as pale as a ghost's, her pounding heart nearly stopped.

He'd followed her from the ranch?

Tears welled in her eyes, and emotion balled in her throat.

"Molly? Are you okay, honey?" His voice, soft and hesitant, was laden with something akin to fear, which set off a wave of emotion in her.

She tried to speak, but she could hardly even nod. Instead, the tears rolled down her cheeks and she reached for him.

He wrapped his arms around her and carefully helped her from the car. When he'd looked her over for injury and apparently determined she was whole, he said, "Hang on, honey. I need to check the other guy."

She nodded, glad that he was taking charge since her hands were trembling and her legs had turned to mush.

Realizing that they'd need an ambulance, she returned to her car and reached for the cell phone in her purse. The hardest part was urging her uncooperative fingers to dial 911.

Interestingly enough, she had the presence of mind to report the accident, telling the dispatcher which intersection they were in. Apparently medical training trumped fear. At least, it had in this case.

She had no idea how long it was before she heard an ambulance in the distance. Three minutes, maybe?

The driver of a minivan parked across the way jumped out of his car and joined Chase beside the pickup.

Moments later Chase was back at her side. "I'd feel better if you went to the hospital and let a doctor look at that knot on your head."

Molly lifted her hand, felt a lump the size of a walnut. She figured it probably wasn't serious, but she would agree to an examination because of the baby.

One of the paramedics came over to check on her, a guy she'd seen on occasion at the E.R. The other one hurried toward the pickup.

After a couple of moments, the paramedic said, "Why don't we take you to the hospital as a precaution?"

"Okay." She wondered if she should mention the baby to him, but she didn't want to say anything in front of Chase. Not that she was keeping it from him anymore. She just didn't want him learning about it this way.

When the medic went to confer with his partner, Chase reached for Molly's hand, his fingers trembling, too. "You have no idea how scared I was when I realized it was your car in the intersection."

She gave his hand a gentle squeeze. "And you have no idea how surprised I was to see you here. When I left the ranch, I thought—"

"You thought wrong. I don't know how we're going to work this out, Molly, but I swear to you we will. I love you. And when you're not with me, a big part of me goes missing."

"I love you, too. And on the way home I had a chance

to think about a lot of things. I'm sorry I gave you an ultimatum. It wasn't fair. That doesn't mean that I won't be scared out of my mind each time you race, but I'm the one with the problem. And I'm willing to talk to a counselor about it."

He brushed a kiss across her brow. "I've never been afraid of losing anyone before, but I got a taste of what that felt like today. And I promise to try and be sensitive to your fears."

The paramedic, who'd been looking Molly over, returned and said, "I don't think that head injury is serious, but we probably should let a doctor decide."

"Is the other driver okay?" Molly asked.

"We think he may have suffered a seizure, which is why he ran the stop sign. But he's conscious and talking." The paramedic straightened. "The police will be here shortly, and they'll arrange for the vehicles to be towed." He glanced at Chase. "We'll be going to Brighton Valley Medical Center. You can follow us if you want."

Chase appeared hesitant, as if he wasn't sure if he wanted to go. And Molly could understand that, although she really didn't want to be alone right now. Still, she had friends at the hospital, so she wasn't as uneasy as she might have been before.

"I can leave my car here and ride with you in the ambulance," Chase said. "In fact, I'd rather do that."

Just the fact that he understood, that he wanted to help, made her smile. "I'll be okay for the short trip to BVMC."

And she was.

Minutes later, Molly and the other driver, a man in his late fifties, were loaded on gurneys and placed in the ambulance. It was weird being on the receiving end of medical treatment, but her biggest concern was for the baby.

She hadn't been pregnant very long, but she'd already grown comfortable with the idea. And now, knowing that Chase would be a part of her life, she was even more content.

Once they'd gotten to the E.R., Mr. Jennings, the driver of the pickup, was whisked into treatment room one. And Molly was taken to bed three. She wasn't sure where Chase was, but she knew he'd be here. And it gave her a solid sense of peace, a sense of knowing that everything would be okay—one way or another.

As the privacy curtain was drawn back, Betsy approached Molly's bed. "How're you doing?"

"Not too bad. I'm a little shaky. And I'm worried about the baby."

"Are you in pain?"

"No."

"Are you experiencing any bleeding?"

"No, I don't think so."

After a brief exam, Betsy said, "You probably ought to take it easy for a day or two. Maybe go home and put your feet up for the rest of the night. But I think the baby's all right."

"What baby?" Chase asked as he stepped through the gap in the curtains.

Molly turned to face the man she loved, the man with whom she had so much to talk over, so much to decide. "This isn't the way I'd planned to tell you, Chase. But I'm pregnant."

"You are?" Confusion danced across his face. "When…?"

"The first time, I think."

"But how…?"

"Who knows how it happened?"

Betsy chuckled softly. "I've got a pretty good idea how it happened."

Chase didn't seem to catch the humor, as he furrowed his brow, apparently taking it all in.

"I know this is a bit sudden and unexpected for you to wrap your mind around," Molly said. "So if you're not up to being a father, I'll love the baby enough for both of us."

"It's not that," he said. "I'm just…speechless, I guess. But don't worry about loving the baby for the two of us." He lifted her hand and pressed a kiss along the top of her knuckles. "I'm going to be the best father a kid ever had."

Then, bending over her, he kissed her to seal the deal.

When the paperwork had been completed, and a co-payment had been made, Molly was sent home.

"I'll bring the car around," Chase said. "Are you going to be okay with that?"

She knew he was talking about her riding with him, and she appreciated the fact that he understood. "Yes, I'll be all right."

He took her by the hand and led her out the main entrance of the E.R., then stopped by a bench that was near the automatic doors. "Wait here for me. I won't be long."

"Betsy gave me the name of a counselor," she said, as she took a seat. "I'm going to call and make an appointment in the morning."

He nodded, as if pondering the wisdom in the statement, but she knew that he agreed. It was the right thing to do, the only thing to do.

"I don't want the baby to grow up to share my fear," she added. "I've got to learn to let go, to trust that things will be all right."

"I'll do everything in my power to always keep you and the baby safe." Chase placed a hand on her cheek, and his gaze locked onto hers. "I think it might be a good idea if I talked to that counselor, too—at least, once or twice. I've been trying to prove something my entire life, something that was proven a long time ago."

Molly placed her hand over his, holding it against her face. Holding the bond that drew them together.

"For what it's worth," Chase said, "I've decided not to drive for Gerald anymore."

"I hate doing that to you. I don't want you to end up resenting me. Or resenting the baby."

"Right now, I can't imagine that happening, Molly. I love you too much. And to be honest, just because I quit driving for Gerald doesn't mean I'll stop racing altogether. I could be offered another opportunity, and I might take it. That's a decision I'll have to make, although I'll consider your feelings when I do. But for now, let's just take things one step at a time." Chase removed his hand from her cheek, then took off into the parking lot.

Minutes later, he returned with the Corvette, the roar of the engine echoing in the night air.

Molly was a little shaky climbing into the sports car, but she buckled up and settled into her seat. And this time, instead of hugging the door, she made a concentrated effort to look straight ahead, to relax and to place herself in Chase's hands.

She also chose to believe that he would do what he said he would, that he would watch out for her safety, as well as the baby's.

When they arrived at her house, he parked in the driveway, then got out of the car and opened the passenger door for her. He reached out a hand, and she took it.

For the first time in her life, Molly felt as though she'd truly come home. The fears might remain a part of her for a while, but with Chase by her side, she knew she could tackle anything.

"I've got an idea," Chase said, as they walked to the door.

"What's that?"

"After you're off bed rest, I'm going to take you out on the road and teach you some defensive driving skills to help you feel more in control of the car."

"I'd like that."

She reached into her purse and withdrew the keys to the door. Then she handed them to him and waited for him to let them inside.

"I'll take care of feeding Rusty," he said. "Why don't you lie down and put your feet up like Dr. Nielson said."

"All right."

He led her into the bedroom and pulled back the covers. "You're in good hands with me, Molly."

"I know." She offered him a warm smile, then, while he went to take care of the cat, she undressed and put on a clean nightgown.

She'd no more than climbed into bed when he returned.

"I'm staying tonight," he said.

She smiled. "I'm glad."

"And I'm going to sleep with you," he said. "But I won't touch you. I won't hurt you. I just want to be with you and the baby."

"You're going to have to touch me a little," she said, her eyes surely glimmering. "I sleep better when I'm wrapped in your arms."

His smile could have lit a darkened room. "I don't know what the future will bring, Molly. But I love you. And no matter what happens, we're going to be in it together."

He had that right.

She lifted her arms, silently inviting him into her bed, into her life, into her future.

# *Epilogue*

Molly stood before the mirror in the choir room of the Brighton Valley Community Church, adjusting her veil and making a last-minute check of her hair and dress.

She noted the definite baby bump that stretched the front of her gown and couldn't help running her hand along the bulge where her son or daughter grew. She'd tried to talk Chase into flying to Las Vegas to get married, just so she wouldn't look like a blimp dressed in white lace, but he'd refused to hear of it.

"You look beautiful pregnant," he'd said. "And I want you to have a real wedding."

Betsy, who'd agreed to be her maid of honor, approached holding the bridal bouquet. "It's time to go. Are you ready?"

Molly turned to face her friend and smiled. "Sometimes it's hard to believe that I'm going to be a wife and mother."

"If there's anyone who deserves to be happy and to have a family of her own, it's you, Molly." Betsy gave her a hug, then handed her the bouquet of tulips, the stems bound together with a satin ribbon.

"Thanks. You deserve someone special in your life, too, Betsy."

"Don't worry about me. I have the hospital, my colleagues and my patients, so my life is full. Besides, I made a big mistake trusting the wrong man once before, and I'm not going to risk making another one."

"I've been learning a lot about risks lately," Molly said. "And I'm beginning to realize that life was meant to be lived."

"Sounds like you've been listening to the therapist."

"Actually," Molly said as she turned away from the mirror, "she's given me some things to think about, as well as some tools that are working. But the person who has really made the biggest difference in my life and my attitude has been Chase. I don't know if I told you this, but he's been giving me driving lessons. He even took me to the race track the other day and had me make a few laps."

"Don't tell me you're going to take up racing," the E.R. doctor said, a grin stretching across her face.

Molly laughed. "No, of course not. But I do feel more competent behind the wheel now. I know that I'm in good hands when he drives, too."

"I'm so happy things are working out so well."

"Sometimes you just have to choose to trust someone, and I can't think of a better person to trust than Chase."

"Then let's not keep him waiting." Betsy opened the door and led Molly to the back of the small church, where their family and friends waited.

The pews were filled, the altar adorned with blue and white hydrangeas.

Molly was sorry her parents and brother weren't able to be with her today, but her grandmother, who had been seated in the front row, had made it. And on top of that, Chase's family had been wonderful. Both Molly and Grandma had been welcomed into the fold.

Betsy nodded to the wedding coordinator, who in turn told the organist to start the music. Moments later, after Betsy started the march, Molly fell into step behind her. Everyone's eyes were on Molly, but all she could do was to look at her groom, the man she would pledge her heart and her very life to.

Chase stood as handsome as he'd ever been, his dark hair stylishly mussed, cheeks dimpled with a smile, eyes glimmering with what could only be love.

Molly thought her heart would surely burst. She'd been given a second chance to have a family, and she was going to rise and snatch it, grasping the opportunity like the brass ring on a merry-go-round.

As she reached the front of the church, the minister didn't ask who gave her away. She and Chase had decided earlier that she would come to him freely and on her own, making a conscious decision to trust him with her heart.

Chase reached out his hand, and she took it.

"I love you," he whispered.

"I love you, too."

They turned to face the altar.

"Dearly beloved," the minister began as he joined their hearts and their lives forever.

The service was short and sweet, and when they were pronounced husband and wife, they sealed their vows with a warm and loving kiss.

Molly didn't know what the future would hold, but whatever happened, they would face it together.

The racing season had started already, and while several sponsors had approached Chase about driving their cars, he'd passed on it.

"I'm not saying I'll never race again," he'd told Molly after the last offer, "but the truth is, I'm not sure it's what I really want to do. And I'm not going to rush back into a situation where I have to live under someone's thumb."

Instead, he'd talked about opening a driving school for kids who wanted to compete on the youth circuit, utilizing the style and technique his father had taught him. The response had been tremendous, and even Chase's dad had gotten excited about the idea.

Interestingly, the two men had become closer than they'd ever been, and Phil was eager to offer advice and guidance to Chase, who'd gladly accepted it.

Now, as Molly and Chase made their way into the fellowship hall, where the reception would take place, he gave her hand a squeeze. "I can't wait to start our lives together."

"Neither can I." Then she turned and wrapped her arms around his neck, kissing him with all the love, all the hope in her heart. And at that very moment she knew without a doubt that love would see them through.

* * * * *

*Don't miss the next book in*
*Judy Duarte's new miniseries*
**BRIGHTON VALLEY MEDICAL CENTER**
*Coming in 2010*
*Available wherever Silhouette books are sold*

*Celebrate Harlequin's 60th anniversary with
Harlequin® Superromance®
and the DIAMOND LEGACY miniseries!*

*Follow the stories of four cousins as they come to
terms with the complications of love and what it means
to be a family. Discover with them the sixty-year-old
secret that rocks not one but two families in...
A DAUGHTER'S TRUST by Tara Taylor Quinn.*

*Available in September 2009 from
Harlequin® Superromance®*

RICK'S APPOINTMENT with his attorney early Wednesday morning went only moderately better than his meeting with social services the day before. The prognosis wasn't great—but at least his attorney was going to file a motion for DNA testing. Just so Rick could petition to see the child…his sister's baby. The sister he didn't know he had until it was too late.

The rest of what his attorney said had been downhill from there.

Cell phone in hand before he'd even reached his Nitro, Rick punched in the speed dial number he'd programmed the day before.

Maybe foster parent Sue Bookman hadn't received his message. Or had lost his number. Maybe she didn't want to talk to him. At this point he didn't much care what she wanted.

"Hello?" She answered before the first ring was complete. And sounded breathless.

Young and breathless.

"Ms. Bookman?"

"Yes. This is Rick Kraynick, right?"

"Yes, ma'am."

"I recognized your number on caller ID," she said,

her voice uneven, as though she was still engaged in whatever physical activity had her so breathless to begin with. "I'm sorry I didn't get back to you. I've been a little...distracted."

The words came in more disjointed spurts. Was she jogging?

"No problem," he said, when, in fact, he'd spent the better part of the night before watching his phone. And fretting. "Did I get you at a bad time?"

"No worse than usual," she said, adding, "Better than some. So, how can I help?"

God, if only this could be so easy. He'd ask. She'd help. And life could go well. At least for one little person in his family.

It would be a first.

"Mr. Kraynick?"

"Yes. Sorry. I was...are you sure there isn't a better time to call?"

"I'm bouncing a baby, Mr. Kraynick. It's what I do."

"Is it Carrie?" he asked quickly, his pulse racing.

"How do you know Carrie?" She sounded defensive, which wouldn't do him any good.

"I'm her uncle," he explained, "her mother's— Christy's—older brother, and I know you have her."

"I can neither confirm nor deny your allegations, Mr. Kraynick. Please call social services." She rattled off the number.

"Wait!" he said, unable to hide his urgency. "Please," he said more calmly. "Just hear me out."

"How did you find me?"

"A friend of Christy's."

"I'm sorry I can't help you, Mr. Kraynick," she said softly. "This conversation is over."

"I grew up in foster care," he said, as though that gave him some special privilege. Some insider's edge.

"Then you know you shouldn't be calling me at all."

"Yes... But Carrie is my niece," he said. "I need to see her. To know that she's okay."

"You'll have to go through social services to arrange that."

"I'm sure you know it's not as easy as it sounds. I'm a single man with no real ties and I've no intention of petitioning for custody. They aren't real eager to give me the time of day. I never even knew Carrie's mother. For all intents and purposes, our mother didn't raise either one of us. All I have going for me is half a set of genes. My lawyer's on it, but it could be weeks— months—before this is sorted out. Carrie could be adopted by then. Which would be fine, great for her, but then I'd have lost my chance. I don't want to take her. I won't hurt her. I just have to see her."

"I'm sorry, Mr. Kraynick, but..."

\* \* \* \* \*

*Find out if Rick Kraynick will ever have
a chance to meet his niece.
Look for A DAUGHTER'S TRUST
by Tara Taylor Quinn,
available in September 2009.*

**We'll be spotlighting a different series
every month throughout 2009
to celebrate our 60th anniversary.**

**Look for Harlequin® Superromance®
in September!**

*Celebrate with
The Diamond Legacy
miniseries!*

Follow the stories of four cousins as they come to terms
with the complications of love and what it means to
be a family. Discover with them the sixty-year-old secret
that rocks not one but two families.

**A DAUGHTER'S TRUST** by *Tara Taylor Quinn*
**September**

**FOR THE LOVE OF FAMILY** by *Kathleen O'Brien*
**October**

**LIKE FATHER, LIKE SON** by *Karina Bliss*
**November**

**A MOTHER'S SECRET** by *Janice Kay Johnson*
**December**

**Available wherever books are sold.**

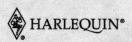

# HARLEQUIN®

## *American ★ Romance*®

# The Ranger's Secret
## REBECCA WINTERS

When Yosemite Park ranger Chase Jarvis rescues
an injured passenger from a downed helicopter,
he is stunned to discover it's the woman he
once loved. But Chase is no longer the man
Annie Bower knew. Will she forgive him for
the secret he's been keeping for ten long years?
And will he forgive Annie for her own secret—
the daughter Chase didn't know he had…?

*Available September
wherever books are sold.*

## "LOVE, HOME & HAPPINESS"

www.eHarlequin.com

HAR75279

# You're invited to join our Tell Harlequin Reader Panel!

By joining our new reader panel you will:

- Receive Harlequin® books—they are FREE and yours to keep with no obligation to purchase anything!
- Participate in fun online surveys
- Exchange opinions and ideas with women just like you
- Have a say in our new book ideas and help us publish the best in women's fiction

*In addition, you will have a chance to win great prizes and receive special gifts! See Web site for details. Some conditions apply. Space is limited.*

## To join, visit us at
# www.TellHarlequin.com.

# REQUEST YOUR FREE BOOKS!

## 2 FREE NOVELS PLUS 2 FREE GIFTS!

# SPECIAL EDITION®

## Life, Love and Family!

**YES!** Please send me 2 FREE Silhouette Special Edition® novels and my 2 FREE gifts (gifts are worth about $10). After receiving them, if I don't wish to receive any more books, I can return the shipping statement marked "cancel." If I don't cancel, I will receive 6 brand-new novels every month and be billed just $4.24 per book in the U.S. or $4.99 per book in Canada. That's a savings of at least 15% off the cover price! It's quite a bargain! Shipping and handling is just 50¢ per book.* I understand that accepting the 2 free books and gifts places me under no obligation to buy anything. I can always return a shipment and cancel at any time. Even if I never buy another book from Silhouette, the two free books and gifts are mine to keep forever.

235 SDN EYN4  335 SDN EYPG

Name _____ (PLEASE PRINT)

Address _____ Apt. #

City _____ State/Prov. _____ Zip/Postal Code

Signature (if under 18, a parent or guardian must sign)

### Mail to the **Silhouette Reader Service:**
**IN U.S.A.:** P.O. Box 1867, Buffalo, NY 14240-1867
**IN CANADA:** P.O. Box 609, Fort Erie, Ontario L2A 5X3

Not valid to current subscribers of Silhouette Special Edition books.

**Want to try two free books from another line?**
**Call 1-800-873-8635 or visit www.morefreebooks.com.**

* Terms and prices subject to change without notice. Prices do not include applicable taxes. Sales tax applicable in N.Y. Canadian residents will be charged applicable provincial taxes and GST. Offer not valid in Quebec. This offer is limited to one order per household. All orders subject to approval. Credit or debit balances in a customer's account(s) may be offset by any other outstanding balance owed by or to the customer. Please allow 4 to 6 weeks for delivery. Offer available while quantities last.

**Your Privacy:** Silhouette is committed to protecting your privacy. Our Privacy Policy is available online at www.eHarlequin.com or upon request from the Reader Service. From time to time we make our lists of customers available to reputable third parties who may have a product or service of interest to you. If you would prefer we not share your name and address, please check here. ☐

SSE09R

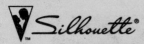

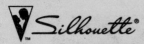Silhouette®

# COMING NEXT MONTH
## Available August 25, 2009

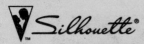SPECIAL EDITION

### #1993 TEXAS CINDERELLA—Victoria Pade
*The Foleys and the McCords*
When Tate McCord caught reporter Tanya Kimbrough snooping around the McCord mansion for business secrets, he had to admit—the housekeeper's daughter had become a knockout! The real scoop—this Texas Cinderella was about to steal the surgeon's heart.

### #1994 A MARRIAGE-MINDED MAN—Karen Templeton
*Wed in the West*
Lasting relationships had never been in the cards for single mom Tess Montaya. But when her teenage sweetheart, Eli Garrett, reentered her life, it looked as if this time they were playing for keeps. Could the carpenter and the Realtor build a home…together?

### #1995 THE PREGNANT BRIDE WORE WHITE—
Susan Crosby
*The McCoys of Chance City*
When Keri Overton came to Chance City to tell Jake McCoy he was going to be a daddy, he wasn't there. But the town gave her such a warm welcome, she stayed…until Jake returned, in time for nine-months-pregnant Keri to make an honest man of him.

### #1996 A COLD CREEK HOMECOMING—RaeAnne Thayne
*The Cowboys of Cold Creek*
Home visiting his ailing mother, CEO Quinn Sutherland was shocked to find snooty ol' Tess Clayborne caring for her. In high school, Quinn had thought the homecoming queen was stuck up—but now he found the softer, gentler woman irresistible….

### #1997 BABY BY SURPRISE—Karen Rose Smith
*The Baby Experts*
As a neonatologist, Francesca Talbot knew a thing or two about babies—until it came to her own difficult pregnancy. That's when she turned to the child's father, rancher Grady Fitzgerald, to provide shelter in the storm…and a love to last a lifetime.

### #1998 THE HUSBAND SHE COULDN'T FORGET—
Carmen Green
Abandoned by her husband, Melanie Bishop took a job as a therapist…and immediately fell for her amnesiac patient Rolland Jones, whom a car accident had transformed inside and out. What was it about Rolland that reminded her so of the husband she'd loved?

SSECNMBPA0809